Elizabeth Gail
and the
Holiday
Mystery

Hilda Stahl

Tyndale House Publishers, Inc., Wheaton, Illinois

6872

Dedicated with love to
Tom, Judy, and Rachel Hicks

The Elizabeth Gail Series

Cover and interior illustration by Kathy Kulin

Library of Congress Catalog Card Number 88-51709
ISBN 0-8423-0802-4
Copyright © 1982 by Word Spinners, Inc.
Printed in the United States of America

95 94 93
10 9 8 7 6 5 4

Contents

ONE
Ice-skating

The cold air turned Libby's cheeks and nose red as she skated slowly and awkwardly after Jill. Libby sighed and shook her head. Would she ever learn to ice-skate well? She was not little Libby Dobbs anymore, but Elizabeth Gail Johnson, and in two and a half months she'd be fourteen years old.

Her ankle twisted and she plopped to the ice, her arms flailing wildly. Her red and white jacket felt too hot and her ski pants too tight. Had anyone seen her fall?

"Are you hurt, Elizabeth? Let me help you."

She looked up and her heart skipped a beat. Why did it have to be Scott Norris of all people? "I'm all right, Scott."

He caught her firmly and lifted her up and her breath caught in her throat. "I'll skate with you awhile, Elizabeth."

Oh, dear! What could she do now? She could not skate with Scott Norris! "I'll be all right, Scott." She tried to pull away, but his grip was strong.

"That was a nasty fall, Elizabeth." He smiled down at

her and she frowned. Did he notice how fast her heart was beating? "Where's your friend Jill? I'll skate you to her and then you'll feel better."

Did he think she was a baby? "I don't need anyone to hold on to me. I can skate."

He laughed and the sound sent pleasant shivers up and down her back. "If you could skate as well as you play the piano, then I wouldn't have to worry about you at all."

"Do you really like my playing?" she asked breathlessly, her hazel eyes wide.

He nodded. "I heard you again yesterday. Chuck and Vera had told us about your talent, but I didn't think a little girl could play so well."

"I'm not a little girl! I'm almost fourteen years old!" Did he think because he was nineteen he was a man?

Scott laughed again and she frowned. "You *are* growing up, Elizabeth. Maybe I'll come back in five years and visit the Johnson family again."

She wanted to tell him that she hoped he'd come back much, much sooner than that, but she only smiled a small, tight smile and tugged to get away. He must not know that she liked him as much as she did. He might laugh at her.

Shouts from others on the rink filled the air, startling Libby. For a minute it had seemed as if she and Scott were the only people on the rink. But Susan was skating just a short distance away with Joe Wilkens, and Toby and Kevin were playing their own form of ice hockey with a bunch of boys. Even Ben had been able to get away from his Christmas tree business long enough to ice-skate.

"Here comes Jill," said Scott.

Jill stopped herself with a spray of ice in front of them and looked questioningly at Libby. "I thought you were right behind me."

Libby flushed. "I fell down."

Jill lifted an eyebrow and Libby was afraid of what she was going to say next. Jill was the only person alive who knew how she felt about Scott Norris. It would be absolutely terrible if she even hinted to Scott.

"I didn't get hurt," said Libby quickly.

"I'll leave you girls now. If you need my help, just call." Scott smiled and skated gracefully away. He stopped beside a girl and Libby saw it was Joanne Tripper. Libby frowned, then turned abruptly away. She could not watch Scott with Joanne Tripper!

Jill laughed softly. "If looks could kill, then Joanne would be dead." Jill caught Libby's arm and skated slowly away from the group of noisy boys. "Why didn't you keep Scott with you, Libby?"

Libby shook her head hard. "I couldn't skate at all if he was beside me!"

Jill nudged Libby playfully. "I thought you didn't like boys. I thought you were so busy studying to be a concert pianist that you didn't have time to fall in love."

Libby looked down at the skate marks on the ice so Jill couldn't see her blush. She shrugged her slender shoulders. "Who says I'm in love? I only *like* him." She looked up at Jill who was a half a head taller. "I don't love him the way you do Adam Feuder."

Jill squeezed Libby's arm tightly. "Did you know that Adam came over last night and played chess with me?"

Libby stared in surprise and shook her head. "He did?"

Jill flushed. "I think he likes me a little."

"Will you be so busy with Adam that you won't have

time to write your book?" Libby skated around two small girls. "Maybe you'll want Adam for your best friend instead of me."

Jill shook her head, her brown eyes serious. Brown curls framed her round face. "You'll always be my very best friend, Libby."

Libby smiled as they skated side by side. She remembered how terrible it had felt to be an ugly aid kid nobody wanted. Then she hadn't had any friends. Now, she had friends and a real family who loved her. She looked across the pond at Susan. Susan was her sister now, and Ben, Toby, and Kevin were her brothers. She smiled contentedly; then the smile froze on her face. She clutched at Jill's arm. "Look at those mean boys! They're making Toby cry. I'm going to see what's happening."

"I'll come with you. I think my little brother is teasing Toby, too."

Libby slid to an awkward stop beside Toby. She looked at his flushed face. It was so red that his freckles didn't show. "What's wrong, Toby?"

"Tell her, crybaby," said one of the boys, laughing hard.

Toby doubled his fists, then plopped on the ice and the boys laughed.

Libby bent to help him up, but he slapped her hands away and struggled to his feet. He glared at the boy laughing the hardest. "Greg, don't you say another thing about Goosy Poosy!" cried Toby.

"What about Goosy Poosy?" asked Libby with a frown. Why would the boys be talking about the Johnsons' pet goose?

"We're going to steal him and eat him for Christmas dinner," said Greg loudly.

Toby lunged at Greg and knocked him to the ice. "You can't hurt my goose! You leave my goose alone!"

Before Libby could move, Scott pulled the boys apart, then stood with his arm around Toby.

"You boys came to play, not fight," said Scott sharply.

"They said they're going to eat Goosy Poosy for Christmas dinner," said Toby with a catch in his voice.

"They're teasing," said Scott sharply.

"That is no way to tease," said Libby, glaring at the boys. "Get away from my brother."

Greg skated backwards and laughed again. "He's not your brother. He's adopted and so are you. You don't really belong anywhere."

Libby glanced quickly at Scott, her face on fire. Did he think she really didn't belong to the Johnson family even though they had adopted her several months ago?

Scott turned with Toby and skated away. Libby looked after him, as tears pricked her eyes and a hard lump formed in her throat. Someone bumped against her and she clutched for Jill's arm, then turned as Joanne Tripper tipped back her head and laughed. Her long blonde hair hung down her back almost to her narrow waist. A light green hat sat on her head and a matching scarf was draped around her neck.

"How can you leave your piano long enough to ice-skate?" asked Joanne mockingly.

Libby bit the inside of her bottom lip and looked away.

"I think you should get away from us," said Jill sternly. "All you ever do is cause trouble."

Joanne opened her blue eyes wide. "Me? I don't cause the trouble. Libby does! Everywhere she goes, she makes trouble."

Libby doubled her fists as Jill's grip on her arm

12

tightened. "Let's get out of here, Jill," said Libby harshly.

"You shouldn't be allowed in the park or on the ice," said Joanne sharply. "And neither should that ragged Carrie Brown."

Libby glanced at the thin girl sliding across the ice on her tennis shoes. Carrie Brown was just the type of girl that Joanne would pick on. Libby wanted to skate after Joanne and knock her flat on the ice. Instead Libby turned away and skated to the edge of the rink with Jill. Libby brushed her mittened hand across her face. She was a Christian and she couldn't go around knocking people down, not even rotten girls like Joanne Tripper.

"Elizabeth, it's time to go home," said Scott from the bench beside the rink where he sat with Toby. "I told your mom I'd have you home by four so we can do chores."

Libby nodded as she stumbled to another bench and sat down. Her fingers felt cold and numb as she untied her skates. Maybe if she worked it right, she could sit beside Scott on the way home. Her skin pricked with heat. She wasn't lovesick like Susan or Jill. She had more important things to think about. She peeked over at Scott, then down at her feet as she pulled her boots on.

TWO
Strange visitor

Libby stood beside the barn and watched Ben and Adam hitch Jack and Dan to the wagon. Scott walked around the wagon and stopped at Dan's head. Libby's heart raced. Scott looked very handsome in his blue jacket. She knew the jacket was just the color of his eyes. His dark brown hair looked almost black. Did he know she was watching him? She stepped back quickly and pressed against the side of the barn.

Goosy Poosy honked and ran to Scott. He didn't back away, but held out his arms and the big white goose rubbed his head up and down Scott's arm. Libby sighed and pushed her mittened hands under her arms. Why couldn't she run to the wagon and tell Ben that she was going with him and his customer to choose a Christmas tree? Two years ago when she'd first come to the Johnson farm she'd helped him with his Christmas tree business. She bit the inside of her bottom lip. With Scott here, she wanted to go again. She wanted to be with him as much as possible for the next two weeks that he was staying with them.

"Who's your customer today?" Libby heard Scott ask Ben.

"The Tripper family. I think you know Joanne Tripper." Ben stood at Jack's head beside Scott. Ben was almost as tall as Scott.

Libby frowned, her eyes narrowing. Joanne Tripper! She had probably talked her parents into getting their Christmas tree from Ben just because of Scott. Would Scott enjoy riding beside Joanne back to the Christmas trees? Libby's heart beat faster and she wanted to run to Scott and beg him to stay home and talk with her. She shook her head. She couldn't do that or he might guess how she felt about him.

"Here comes your customer now," said Adam.

"I'll lock Goosy Poosy up," said Ben. "He sometimes acts too friendly."

Libby rolled her eyes as she remembered the first day that Miss Miller had brought her to the Johnson farm. Miss Miller had stood beside her car, talking to Vera about her visiting routine for foster children, while the big white goose had flapped his long wings and stuck out his long neck and honked his terrible honk. Libby shivered as she remembered how frightening it had been to be knocked down by the goose. Later Kevin had told her that if she hadn't kicked at him he wouldn't have knocked her down.

Jack nickered and shook his head up and down. The bells on the harness jingled musically. Quickly Libby pressed tighter against the side of the barn. Joanne would say something embarrassing if she saw Libby watching.

Mrs. Tripper laughed as she walked toward the wagon. Libby frowned. Mrs. Tripper was probably making fun of everything. She stopped beside the wagon and her husband helped her in. Libby stepped further into the shadow of the barn so Mrs. Tripper wouldn't see her. She didn't want to hear again how unfair it was that she was succeeding at piano when it should have been the precious Joanne Tripper. Libby shook her head. For over a year now Mrs. Tripper had been trying to find ways to get Libby to give up her piano lessons with the famous Rachael Avery so that Joanne could take from her. Maybe Mrs. Tripper would give up trying one of these days.

"Are you going to sit with me, Scott?" Libby heard Joanne say in the voice that she used on boys she found attractive. Libby wanted to leap out and yell for Scott to stay away from Joanne, but she forced herself to stand still. Her heart raced and it was hard to breathe.

"Sure, I'll sit with you, Joanne," said Scott. "I want to hear more about your future as a concert pianist. You know that Elizabeth is going to be one, too, don't you?"

"Libby, you mean?" Joanne's voice was cold and hard. "She will never make it. Look at her background. Look at her appearance."

"She'll make it," snapped Ben, and Libby wanted to hug him. He always stuck up for her. "Are you all ready to go?" He slapped the reins and said, "Get up." Jack and Dan pulled together and the wagon rolled out of the yard to the pasture. Rex barked and tugged against his chain. He usually ran along beside the wagon, but Mrs. Tripper had said that she was allergic to dogs. She probably just wanted to show Ben she was the boss.

Libby watched until the wagon rolled out of sight behind a hill, then pushed herself away from the barn. Snowball nickered and Rex barked. Libby looked at him with a smile. He was probably asking her to come pet him. But Rex seemed tense, and his barking was interrupted by a low, menacing growl.

"What is he barking at?" Libby wondered. Rex was not looking her way, but he was looking toward the chicken house. A rooster crowed and Goosy Poosy honked indignantly, the way he always did when he was locked up. But Rex was not barking at them.

Something moved near a tree and Libby froze in her tracks. It couldn't be Mother trying to kidnap her again after all these months, could it? Libby shivered and wrapped her arms against herself. Mother had not tried to see her or talk to her since the time that terrible man had kidnapped her and locked her in. She wouldn't come back to this area, would she? The police were probably still looking for her.

Rex barked again and Libby looked quickly across the yard to the large white house. Could she make it to the back door before anyone grabbed her? She swallowed hard, her eyes wide with fear.

Another flash of color among the trees caught her eye and she strained to see. Who was running away from the farm buildings, and why?

Slowly Libby walked toward the chicken house. It couldn't be Mother. She wouldn't run into the woods. She'd run toward the road and a car.

Maybe it was Kevin or Toby playing a spy game. Libby sighed in relief at the thought. Sure, it had to be one of them. Well, it was too cold to play such childish games today. She'd fool them and just go into the house and practice her piano. This morning's lesson was a little harder than last week's. It would take several hours of practice to get it the way Rachael Avery wanted it.

The warmth in the house felt good to Libby as she tugged off her boots and coat. She rubbed her hand down Chuck's big red plaid farm coat and remembered the time she'd hidden behind it with Ben and Kevin standing in front of her to give Chuck a surprise when he came home from working in his store in town. Oh, but she was glad that Chuck was her father now!

Sounds of the TV from the family room and soft music from Chuck's study drifted into the hall. Libby stopped outside the living room and looked at the tall Christmas tree that they'd cut and decorated last week. She sniffed and closed her eyes. The pine smell was wonderful!

Just then Libby heard Susan laugh; then Joe joined in. Libby knew they were in the basement playing Ping-Pong. Chuck and Vera had said that Joe could visit twice a week to see Susan. Libby sighed as she pushed her hands into her jeans pockets. It would be heavenly if Scott lived nearby so that he could visit twice a week. His college was too far away. At least he was spending his Christmas break with them since his parents were in Florida.

Libby stopped in the family room door, then gasped, her hand at her mouth. Toby and Kevin were both watching TV!

Who had been running through the trees?

A shiver slithered down Libby's spine and she hurried to the study to find Vera. Maybe she knew. The study was empty and Libby hurried to the kitchen. Vera looked up from where she sat at the table with a cup of tea and a book. Her blonde hair curled prettily around her face.

"What's wrong, Elizabeth?" she asked, her blue eyes wide. "You look upset."

Libby rubbed her hand across her soft sweatshirt. "I just saw someone in our yard and I thought it was one of the boys, but they're both watching TV. I don't know who was out there! Maybe Mother!" She knew she sounded frantic, but the thought of having Mother sneaking around terrified her.

"Sit down, Libby." Vera pushed out a chair and Libby thankfully sank down on it, her icy hands locked together. "Your mother wouldn't come here. She knows she'd be in trouble if she did. It was probably one of the neighbor children or even a lost hunter."

Libby licked her dry lips and tried to relax. Vera was probably right.

"Did Scott go with Ben?"

Libby nodded.

"I'll miss him when he goes back to school." Vera sipped her tea, then set her cup back on the saucer. "I'm thankful that he came here for his vacation. Chuck and I love him and his family. Scott is like a nephew to us."

"Maybe he'll come stay for the summer, too." Libby tried to appear casual and natural, but it was hard. Could Vera guess how she really felt about Scott?

"He said he might be able to come for a week or so, but he has a summer job lined up at home."

Libby walked to the sink and turned on the cold water. She filled a glass, then drank. Was there any way she could get Scott to find a summer job nearby so he could stay the summer with them?

"Elizabeth, did you practice your piano for the Christmas program tomorrow?"

Libby turned and shook her head. "The boys are watching TV. I could practice later."

"It's time the boys went outdoors and played their

own football game instead of watching it on TV." Vera stood up and tugged her sweater down over her jeans.

Several minutes later Libby sat at the piano and lovingly touched the keys. Someday she'd play for thousands of people and they'd clap and shout for more. Elizabeth Gail Johnson would be a famous concert pianist! She flushed. She was no longer ragged Libby Dobbs, aid kid. She'd been adopted into this family who had prayed her in. She belonged to them and her dreams were coming true! Libby played through the song, "O Come All Ye Faithful," three times, then sat back with her eyes closed. Chuck had said to play the song as her gift to Jesus on his birthday. Libby's heart swelled with love. She loved Jesus and he loved her! She'd play the song to him tomorrow and she'd play her very best! She turned at a sound to find Susan standing in the doorway. "Hi, Susan. Did Joe go home?"

Susan flipped her long red-gold hair over her slender shoulder as she walked to the couch and sat down. "Mom said it was time. I wish I was old enough to get married!"

Libby walked to the fireplace and sat on the raised hearth. Before Scott she'd have thought Susan was dumb, but now she didn't. "At least you get to see Joe every day in school." After Scott went back to college, she wouldn't see him until summer. That was a lifetime away! How could she stand it?

Just then Toby and Kevin burst into the room. Libby saw the excitement on their faces.

"Where's Mom?" asked Kevin, looking around.

"In the study," said Susan. "Why?" She sounded scared.

Kevin turned to leave, but Libby grabbed his arm.

"What's wrong, Kevin?" she asked around the tightness in her throat.

"Someone stole our black and white chicken!" cried Toby, his hazel eyes large.

"What?" cried Susan, leaping up.

Kevin pushed his glasses against his round face and nodded. "It's gone all right and no fox took it or there'd be feathers. Somebody walked right into the pen and took her!"

Libby swallowed hard. Had the person who'd been sneaking around outdoors been the thief? Had she seen the chicken thief without knowing it?

THREE
Christmas program

Libby watched the nursery class walk to the platform for their part in the Christmas program, then peeked over at Scott who sat beside Ben. Libby felt weak as she locked her fingers together in her lap. Scott looked just the way he had last week when he'd first come to visit.

Libby looked away from Scott, but she could still see him in her mind. She smiled dreamily, then pulled her face straight. What if someone saw her smile and knew that she'd been thinking of Scott?

Susan coughed. The nursery class sang "Away in a Manger." Libby thought about the day she'd first seen Scott. The doorbell had rung and she'd been in the hall, so she opened the door. He had stood there dressed in a three-piece pearl gray suit, and he smiled at her.

"You must be the famous Elizabeth Gail Johnson," he had said, his blue eyes full of warmth for her. "I'm very glad I finally got to meet you."

"I'm glad to meet you," she had said in a soft voice that didn't sound like hers at all.

Just then Chuck had stepped out of his study. "Scott!

I'm glad to see you after all this time! Welcome to our house. Make yourself right at home."

Scott had slipped his arm around Libby's shoulders and said, "This beautiful young lady has already made me feel at home."

Libby peeked over at Scott again, then looked quickly away. He thought she was beautiful! He thought she was famous! He did not care that she'd been kicked from foster home to foster home, or that Mother had beaten her and didn't want her or that Dad had deserted her when she was three. Scott thought she was beautiful! Oh, my!

Libby's stomach fluttered and her face felt hot as she remembered the feeling. She rubbed her hands down her soft blue dress and tried to calm down. How could she play the piano if she kept thinking about Scott? She could not make a mistake in front of him!

Just then Mr. Timmerman introduced Libby's song. She glanced at Scott and he smiled and winked. Her legs felt almost too weak to carry her to the baby grand piano at the side of the platform.

Her hands trembled as she placed her music on the piano. A baby cried; then all was quiet. Libby sat down. What was Scott thinking while he was looking at her? Oh, but she must stop thinking of Scott! Chuck had said to play the song as her gift to Jesus.

She touched the keys, then became totally involved with the song. She played the song for Jesus, and she knew she was playing her best.

She touched the last note, then slowly stood up and smiled at everyone as Rachael Avery had taught her to do. She tried to keep from looking at Scott, but she couldn't stop herself. She looked at him, and he was applauding with the others and smiling right at her as if he were proud of her. Her heart beat faster as she walked back to her seat. Could she walk past Scott without stumbling and falling?

He moved his legs and she started past him. He caught her hand and squeezed it. "That's my girl," he whispered.

She finally sank down in her seat, trembling and hot. Had Scott really called her his girl? Did that mean he liked her as much as she liked him? How could he? She frowned and shook her head slightly. No. He didn't like her that way. She might as well stop thinking he did. She looked down at her clasped hands and forced back tears.

Vera leaned toward Libby. "Anything wrong, honey?"

Libby forced a smile and shook her head. What on earth had she been doing to herself? She had no time to fall for a boy, not even one like Scott Norris! She was going to be a famous concert pianist! Nothing would stop her from fulfilling her dream! She lifted her chin high and squared her shoulders. She would not look at Scott, nor think about him!

As Susan recited her long poem, Libby looked across the aisle, then stared in surprise. Carrie Brown sat beside Mrs. Keeler. Carrie had never been in church before. Libby was glad that Joanne Tripper wasn't here to say something about Carrie's ragged blouse and pants. Carrie sat looking straight ahead, her chin up. Her brown hair was unbrushed and oily. Had Carrie Brown ever been to a church before?

After the closing prayer Mr. Timmerman said, "We have a Christmas treat for everyone. The ushers will stand at the back door and give each one the usual bag of candy, nuts, and fruit. Have a very merry Christmas. We'll see you next Sunday."

Libby looked around at the mad scramble of children heading for the back door. A piece of chocolate candy would taste very good. She looked quickly at Scott, but he was talking with Ben and didn't see her look at him. Would Scott think she was childish if she rushed back to get in line for a treat?

Just then someone caught her arm, and she turned her head to find her Sunday school teacher smiling at her.

"Hi, Connie," said Libby. Had Connie seen her look at Scott?

"Libby, you played beautifully! I want to go to your next recital if I may." Connie pushed a stray strand of dark hair away from her face. She looked very pretty in her red dress.

"I'd like to have you go," said Libby, beaming with pride. "It's in February."

"And in February you'll be fourteen, won't you, Libby?" Libby nodded.

Connie laughed her musical laugh. "I can easily remember your birthday since it's on Valentine's Day."

Libby smiled. Just last year after her birthday she'd been legally adopted by the Johnson family. Now she belonged to them forever!

"You're growing up, Libby."

She flushed with pleasure. "But I hope I don't get any taller." Since last year she'd grown three inches. She would never be short and cute like Susan.

"You have a nice Christmas, Libby." Connie squeezed her arm and hurried away, then stopped to talk to Carrie Brown.

Libby walked toward the back of the church, looking

quickly for Scott. Finally she saw him with Chuck and Vera near the drinking fountain. Libby hesitated. Should she walk back with them? Would Scott praise her playing again? Her stomach fluttered.

Suddenly someone bumped against Libby and she staggered and almost fell, then caught herself just in time. She frowned as two ragged boys ran away from her, laughing loudly. Had Scott seen her almost fall? She'd like to get hold of those boys and tell them just what she thought of them! She watched them push in line and grab treats, then rush out.

Slowly Libby walked to stand in line. Whoever was watching would never guess that she was anxious for the Christmas treat. She stood very straight with her eyes forward and her chin high. Nobody would know that she couldn't wait to open her bag and take out a piece of cream-filled chocolate candy. Laughter and talking surrounded her, but she kept very quiet.

Suddenly someone bumped her and she fell against an old man who was a stranger to her. She mumbled that she was sorry as she stepped back. Her face was on fire as she glared at the same ragged boys who had bumped into her earlier. Once again they pushed into line and once again accepted treats, then rushed outdoors. Libby narrowed her eyes and pressed her lips tightly together. Someone should talk to those boys and tell them to stop taking treats. Was everyone too busy talking to notice those boys?

Finally Libby stood at the back door. She smiled and said, "Thank you," as Mr. Oosterhouse handed her a bag. She hurried out of the church. Cold air stung her cheeks and she pulled her coat tightly around herself. The bag crackled in her hand and she looked at it with a satisfied smile. The weak winter sun shone against the bag as she carefully opened it. Suddenly, a hand reached out and grabbed the bag. She squealed in surprise, then stared after the ragged boys that had bumped her earlier. How dare they take her treat!

"Come back here!" she cried as she ran after them across the parking lot. It was hard to run in her dress boots. She would catch those boys and teach them that they could not take her treat!

She stepped on a patch of ice and slid, her arms swinging to catch her balance. She ran around a small red car, then grabbed one of the ragged boys. "I want my bag! Give it to me right now!"

He looked at her with a surprised look. "What bag? What are you talking about?"

Libby clenched her free hand and glared at him. "You know what bag."

"I don't have no bag."

"Then the other boy does. Tell him to give it to me or you will be lying in a snowbank with my boot in the middle of your back!"

The other boy jumped around the car and held out the bag. "Take your dumb bag if you want it so bad! Come on, Max. Let's get out of here."

Libby released Max and he ran with the other boy. Libby shook her head impatiently, then stopped when she saw Scott walking toward her. Had he seen and heard what she'd done? Oh, a bag of Christmas treats was not worth this!

Someone called to Scott and he turned away. Libby sighed in relief. Slowly she walked toward the Johnson's station wagon, the bag held tightly in her hand. Why couldn't she remember that she wasn't a tough street kid any longer? What would Scott think of her if he had overheard? A cold band squeezed her heart. She kicked a clump of snow, then stopped. Carrie Brown stood beside a dark blue car with her head down and her shoulders drooping. Libby hesitated, then said, "Hi, Carrie."

Carrie looked up, then down again but not before Libby had seen the tears in her eyes. Why was Carrie crying?

"I'm glad you could come today, Carrie."

"Mrs. Babcock brought us." Carrie pushed her hands into her jeans.

"Where's your Christmas treat?"

Carrie shrugged. "I didn't get one. Somebody said I'm too old." She sounded like she was going to cry.

"But you're my age! You're not too old!" Libby wanted to run in the church and grab a bag for Carrie. How could anyone be so mean to Carrie? Was it because she was ragged and dirty?

"I guess I don't really need a treat. I guess I don't really like candy or nuts or fruit."

Libby looked at the bag in her hand, then finally held it out to Carrie. "Have mine. I want you to. Please."

Carrie looked at her a long time, then slowly took the bag. "Thank you, Libby. Thank you."

Libby smiled as Carrie ran to a car and climbed in. Two ragged boys popped up in the back seat and waved at Libby. She frowned as she realized the boys were with Carrie. Libby shrugged, then started to turn away. She froze, her eyes wide. Carrie was holding up four bags and laughing hard! She made a face at Libby, then slumped down in the front seat.

Libby doubled her fists and glared angrily. Carrie

would not be laughing for long! But before Libby could move, Scott walked up to her.

"It's cold out here, Elizabeth. Let's get to the car. The others are waiting."

Libby bit the inside of her bottom lip as she glared once again at Carrie, then Libby slowly walked beside Scott to the car.

Carrie would be sorry for what she'd done! Someday when Scott wasn't around, Carrie would get just what was coming to her!

FOUR
Sleigh ride

Libby rubbed the snowman that Kevin and Paul Noteboom had built two days ago as she thought about the stolen chicken. Who would steal just one hen? Kevin had said that none of the others were missing this morning. Chuck had said not to worry about it, that maybe the black and white chicken had gotten out and then was caught by a fox.

A car drove past on the road at the end of the long driveway. Jack and Dan nickered and the bells of their harnesses jingled as Chuck and Ben hitched them to the sleigh.

Libby turned, then stopped with a blush. Scott stood just a few feet away and he was looking at her. How long had he been standing there? She managed a smile. "Hi, Scott."

He tugged one of his gloves up as he walked toward her. He stopped beside the snowman. "Is something bothering you, Elizabeth? You looked deep in thought."

"I was worried about the stolen chicken."

He nodded. "So are Kevin and Toby. Toby wanted to

stay home from church this morning just to guard the chicken house." Scott rubbed snow off his sleeve. "Chuck told them to stop worrying. And you should stop worrying, too, Elizabeth. We're going for a sleigh ride today just for fun. How can we have fun if you have a long, sad face?" He tapped the end of her nose with his finger and winked.

She felt weak all over as she said, "I guess I'll have to smile some." Would he sit with her and talk to her the way he had with Joanne Tripper? Just how much had he enjoyed being with Joanne? *She* was pretty. *She* had never been an ugly aid kid with baggy clothes and scraggly hair.

Just then Vera called to Scott and he hurried away to talk to her. Libby looked after him, her hands locked behind her back, her heart racing.

Suddenly Toby rushed at the snowman, his head down. He plowed into the snowman and Libby cried out, grabbing him roughly. The snowman toppled to the ground.

"Toby, what do you think you're doing?" asked Libby sharply.

He jerked away from Libby and stood with his feet apart, his hands on his hips. "I hate that snowman! If I had a friend, I could build a better one."

Libby frowned. "You should have helped Kevin and Paul. Paul is your friend."

Toby made a face. "Paul's not my friend! He and Kevin said I'm a big baby and they never want me around. They won't let me play with them again!"

"They didn't mean it, Toby," said Libby.

"Oh, yeah?"

"I'm your friend." Libby started to slip her arms

around him, but Toby jumped back with an angry scowl.

"Don't mush all over me! I don't want hugs or kisses from you!" Toby turned and ran toward the sleigh, and Libby blinked back the tears that stung her eyes. How could Toby do that to her? She'd only been trying to help him.

Rex barked and ran to Libby, pushing his nose against her.

She knelt beside him and hugged him. "You're my friend, Rex. I love you. Who cares if Toby doesn't like me? I sure don't!" But she did!

Rex squirmed and twisted, then licked Libby's cold face. She laughed and wiped it dry.

"It's time to go, Elizabeth," called Chuck as he climbed in the sleigh.

Libby looked quickly at Scott who was helping Vera in the sleigh. Where would Scott sit?

"Come on, Rex." Libby ran to the sleigh with Rex beside her. Snowball nickered from the pen beside the barn, and Libby waved to her white filly.

"Hurry up, Libby," Toby said impatiently.

"Toby," said Vera in her warning voice.

Toby slumped in the seat beside Susan who sat with her arms folded and her head down. Libby knew that Susan was upset that Joe couldn't come.

Libby scrambled in the sleigh and stumbled against Scott. She mumbled that she was sorry as she fought against blushing a bright red.

"Sit with me," said Scott, patting the seat.

"All right." Had she sounded too breathless? Could he hear her heart racing wildly?

"Get up, Jack, Dan," said Chuck loudly as he slapped the reins on the big grays' backs.

Snow flipped up from the horses' hooves and the bells jingled merrily. Vera started singing "Jingle Bells." Libby heard Scott join in and she did, too, in a soft voice that no one could hear.

Chuck stopped at a gate and Ben jumped out and opened it. Chuck drove through and Ben closed the gate and leaped back in the sleigh, snow falling from his boots.

Ben leaned forward. "Elizabeth, Joanne Tripper asked about you yesterday when they were loading their Christmas tree in their trunk."

Libby twisted around. She saw the twinkle in Ben's eyes. His red hair hung down on his wide forehead. "What did she want?"

Ben grinned. "She asked if my sister, the concert pianist, was in the house practicing the piano. I told them that soon you would be so famous that people would pay to look at the house where you live."

Libby laughed and Scott joined in.

"Ben's right," said Scott, nodding.

Ben sat back and Libby looked wide-eyed at Scott. Was he teasing her?

"You have a dream, Elizabeth." Scott sounded very serious. "You have a dream to be a concert pianist, and you're working to fulfill that dream. You have talent and you are improving your skills with practice. You are determined and dedicated. You *will* be a famous concert pianist, Elizabeth. I know it!"

She clasped her hands in her lap and her eyes sparkled. Both Chuck and Rachael Avery had told her this; now Scott said it, too. "I will play in front of thousands of people and they'll clap and want to hear more."

Scott nodded. "You're right. It will happen, Elizabeth.

Don't let anything stop you from accomplishing what you want to accomplish!"

She looked at him thoughtfully. He sounded very intense. "I won't, Scott. I promise."

He shook his head with a slight smile. "No, you won't, will you?" He turned from her and looked across the field, and she wondered what he was thinking.

Just then Chuck stopped the sleigh and looked back. "Do you see the white-tailed deer near the trees on that hill?" He pointed to his left and Libby looked, then made out the deer. Her breath caught in her throat. Even after living on the Johnson farm for two years, she didn't get tired of seeing deer.

"Oh, my," she said softly.

Scott squeezed her hand. "They're beautiful, aren't they?"

She looked down at his gloved hand over hers and she felt the warmth all through her. Did he do that to Joanne Tripper yesterday when he was riding with her?

Rex barked and chased a rabbit across the pasture. The deer leaped away, their white tails high. The sun shone on the snow, making it sparkle. Chuck slapped the reins and called to Jack and Dan. Libby wanted Scott to hold her hand, but he turned and sat with his hands resting on his legs. Libby peeked at him from under her lashes. Would he notice if she moved closer to him? Oh, what was she thinking? She couldn't do that!

"Here we are," called Chuck as he stopped the sleigh. "All out for a big snowball fight." He laughed as he jumped down. He scooped up a handful of snow and pulled back his hand as he looked at Vera, laughing.

"Don't, Chuck!" Vera jumped out of the sleigh,

laughing and squealing. "I don't want snow down my neck!"

Libby giggled and picked up a handful of snow and packed it into a ball. "Watch out, Dad! Here it comes!"

"Oh, no, you don't!" Scott caught Libby around the waist and swung her around and the snowball fell from her hand. "Nobody can snowball my friend Chuck."

Libby stood very still, her breath caught in her throat. She didn't want Scott to let her go. She wanted to turn in his arms and slip her hands up around his neck. Oh, what was she thinking? She couldn't do such a thing! And if she did, Scott would certainly push her away and laugh at her. She struggled and he released her.

"The sides are drawn!" Scott ran to stand beside Chuck. "Boys against girls!"

"But there are more boys," said Susan, catching Vera's hand and tugging her toward Libby. "Five against three isn't fair!"

"That's too bad," said Chuck, throwing a snowball as he laughed, then dodging behind a large blue spruce. The ball splattered on Vera's arm and she ran for cover behind another tree.

Libby ducked behind a middle-sized blue spruce and waited for a clear view of Scott. She wanted to run to Scott, but she stayed still, the snowball in her hand, her eyes sparkling and her cheeks red.

"Dad! Look, Dad!" shouted Ben, pointing. He sounded very upset.

Libby ran with the others to Ben. What was wrong?

"Look! Someone stole one of my Christmas trees!" Ben stood beside a small stump. "These are the trees for next year. Adam and I have been cutting those in that area." He motioned to his right.

"First a chicken and now a tree," said Kevin, his eyes round behind his glasses. "What kind of thief would do this?"

Libby stepped closer to Scott. Who had cut down the Christmas tree?

FIVE
Toby's friend

Libby walked slowly down the carpeted hallway toward
her bedroom with her English book in her hand. Why
should she have homework tonight of all nights? She
wanted to be with Scott in the family room. She would
play the piano for him and he'd tell her how well she
played and how famous she would be someday.

She stopped just outside her closed door, her head
cocked toward a small noise. Someone was in her room!
How dare anyone be in her very own room without her
permission! She jerked open the door, then stared in
surprise. Toby and a strange boy turned around, and
Toby flushed with guilt.

"We were just looking at things, Libby." Toby backed
away from Libby.

Libby looked at the strange boy again. Why, it was
Max Brown, Carrie's brother! "Get out of my room this
minute! And don't you ever come in here again!"

Max looped his thumbs in his jeans pockets and
grinned at Libby. "I told Carrie I'd let her know what kind
of room you had in this big house with these rich people."

"Get out!" Libby doubled her fists and stepped toward the boys. They darted to the door. "Play outdoors, Toby!"

He stopped at the top of the stairs and glared back at her. "Max is my friend and we'll do just what we want!"

Libby slammed her door shut and locked it. Toby would not get into her room ever again! He'd be very sorry if he did.

Slowly Libby walked to her desk and looked at the puzzle box her real dad had sent her for her twelfth birthday. She picked it up and impatiently rubbed off the fingerprints that Toby and Max had made on it. She stood up her red wastebasket and picked up the wadded papers and dropped them back in. Oh, that Toby! She clenched her fists and pressed her thin lips tightly together. Why couldn't Toby find a nice friend?

Libby opened the drawers of her desk, then shook her head in anger. The papers were scattered with letters out of envelopes and pages of letters just dropped in every which way. Had Toby read the last note from Jill where she had talked about Scott? Oh, no! Toby must not learn of her feelings for Scott! Toby would tell everyone, even Scott himself!

Perspiration dotted Libby's face as she searched for the note. Had Toby taken it from her room? What if he had it this minute and was showing it to Scott? That would be the very worst thing ever!

Libby groaned and covered her face with trembling hands. Was Scott right now reading Jill's note and laughing? Or would it make him angry to think a skinny aid girl could dare fall for him? Should she call Jill and find out what she should do? She dashed to Chuck and Vera's room and picked up the phone, then slammed it down again. Susan was talking with Joe! Why couldn't

Susan stay off the phone? Didn't she know there were others who needed to use it at times?

Libby raced downstairs to the study. She turned the knob, but the door was locked. Libby knew Chuck was still at the store, so it had to be Susan. She knocked and Susan called angrily, "I'm on the phone. I'll be out later."

"I need to use the phone, Susan! I won't be on long." Libby rattled the knob and waited impatiently.

"Go away, Libby! I'm on the phone now!"

Libby took a deep breath and slowly walked away from the study. Unless she wanted to break down the door and fight with Susan, she'd have to wait for the phone.

Slowly Libby walked to the living room. She dare not go in the family room where Scott was.

Libby stood beside the gaily decorated Christmas tree and looked down at the many gifts. One gift was sloppily wrapped and the paper was torn. Who had done that? She knelt down and picked it up. The tag said the gift was to Toby from Ben. Had Toby opened it, then tried to wrap it back up? Would Toby do that? Libby sighed unhappily. The way Toby was acting with his friend Max, he would break any rule without thinking twice.

"Elizabeth Gail! What are you doing?"

Libby leaped up, her face hot as she stared at Vera. "I didn't do it. I found it this way." She quickly dropped the gift and locked her fingers together in front of herself. Vera must not think she would lie!

"Don't look so frightened, Elizabeth. I believe you."

Libby sighed in relief. She didn't want to say she thought Toby and Max had done it. She watched Vera as she looked down at the gifts. She could smell Vera's nice perfume. Did Scott like to smell perfume? How could she think about that when she had important things to worry about? Libby brushed her short hair back and clipped her barrette in place. "Do you want me to wrap the gift again, Mom?"

Vera looked at her and shook her head. "We'll let Dad handle this."

Libby rolled her eyes. That meant a talk in the study for Toby. Max wouldn't even be around to take part of the blame. Well, Toby deserved whatever punishment he would get! And he'd get a whole lot more if he had taken the note from Jill and showed it to Scott!

"I must finish supper, Libby. You practice your piano awhile right now so you'll be free after supper to help with dishes." Vera smiled and walked from the room.

Libby swallowed hard, then took a deep breath and walked out of the living room, down the hall to the family room. Maybe Scott wouldn't be there. Maybe he was outdoors helping Ben finish the chores. Before Libby could walk into the family room she heard Vera scream, "Toby! What are you doing?"

Libby ran to the kitchen. Toby stood on the counter with Max beside him. Toby's face was very red, but Max looked pleased with himself.

"Get down this minute!" Vera pointed to the floor, a stern look on her usually smiling face. "What has happened to you, Toby? Why are you up there where you don't belong?"

He dropped to the floor and Max followed. "I wanted to show Max your good dishes," said Toby with his chin stuck out. "We didn't hurt anything."

Vera caught his arm and pushed him onto a chair. "Toby, you stay there until I say you can get up. Max, it

42

is time for you to go home. Who is picking you up?"

Max shrugged and pushed his hair out of his eyes.

"I'll call your parents and take you home myself."

Libby saw the startled look that Max quickly masked. She frowned thoughtfully. What was Max thinking of now?

"I just remembered that my dad said he'd pick me up at . . ." Max looked at the kitchen clock. "At five-thirty and it's five-thirty right now. I'll wait at the end of the driveway for him. See you in school tomorrow, Toby." Max ran from the kitchen before Toby could say a word.

"I think you should find another friend," said Libby in a low voice.

Toby made a face at her, then looked down at the table, his red hair bright with the kitchen light shining on it.

"What's going on?" asked Scott from the doorway.

Libby didn't want to turn and look at him, but she finally did. He was looking at Vera with a questioning look.

"I just saw that friend of Toby's run back behind the chicken house and disappear in the trees."

Vera frowned and Libby shook her head and sighed. What was Max going to do now?

Vera turned to Toby. "Where does Max live, Toby?"

Toby shrugged, then said, "Somewhere on that dirt road in back of our place."

Vera sighed as she fingered the gold chain around her neck. "I suppose he's walking home since I made him leave. It shouldn't take him long by taking a shortcut through our fields."

"He'll probably never come back," said Toby with a

pout. "I don't have any friends! I might as well be the only kid and never have anyone to play with!"

"Toby, you have friends," said Vera as she sat beside him at the table.

Libby walked from the kitchen away from Toby's sad face. She didn't want to hear him being scolded or talked to or anything. And she didn't want him saying a thing about Jill's note with Scott listening.

A fire blazed invitingly in the fireplace in the family room. Libby stood in front of it and looked at the log crackling behind the screen.

"My parents have a fireplace in their front room," said Scott, and Libby jumped. She'd thought he had stayed in the kitchen.

Libby looked self-consciously at her stocking feet. What could she say to Scott? "Do you have brothers or sisters, Scott?"

"Two sisters and they're both married. They're both as anxious as my parents for me to be a doctor."

Libby looked up in surprise. "Are you going to be a doctor?"

He nodded without enthusiasm.

She frowned. "Don't you want to be?"

He stepped back. "Did I say that?"

"No," she said slowly.

He smiled. "Elizabeth Gail, play the piano for me and don't think about what I want or don't want. Please."

Libby wanted to put her arms around him and hold him, but she walked to the piano and sat down. She lifted her eyes to the song that was open on the piano, and she played her best for Scott to cheer him up.

SIX
The Christmas party

Libby lifted her jacket off the hook, then turned as Ben walked in the back door with a frown.

"Where is Toby?" asked Ben as he stomped the snow off his boots. "It's time to go to Connie's party and we can't find Toby."

"Is he in his room?" Libby zipped her jacket, then reached for her boots.

"He wasn't." Ben sighed impatiently. "I don't know what's wrong with Toby. Something sure is bothering him."

Libby nodded. "I've noticed. After yesterday's trouble with Max Brown, Toby should know to choose his friends more carefully." At least he had not showed Jill's note to Scott or anyone else.

Just then Susan rushed in, her cheeks pink and her blue eyes sparkling. She tugged her white flowered sweater over her new yellow slacks, then reached for her jacket. "Did you find Toby, Ben? I looked all over the house and he's not there. He had better not make us late!"

"I don't know where he is," said Ben, shaking his head.

Susan impatiently lifted her long red-gold hair out of

her collar and flipped it down her back and over her slender shoulders. "Joe will be waiting for me and I will not be late!"

"Mom said for us to get into the car," said Libby. "Toby will come. He won't want to miss the party either." Libby looked wistfully down the hall. How could the party be fun without Scott? What could she do to get to stay home with him?

Reluctantly Libby walked to the car with Ben and Susan. As she reached to open the door, Vera and Kevin hurried out.

"Did you find Toby?" asked Vera in concern.

"No, Mom." Ben looked around the yard lit by the tall yard light. He cupped his hands around his mouth and called, "Toby, we're leaving right now. Come on!"

The back door slammed and Libby turned to find Scott standing there pulling his jacket on. "Do you suppose something happened to Toby?"

Vera frowned. "Toby! Come here right now!"

Just then Toby ran into the lighted part of the yard. He pushed his brown hat back. His red hair looked bright around his pale face. He tugged at the zipper on his snowmobile suit. "I'm not going. You can just leave me home!"

"Will you stop being so dumb and get in the car?" cried Susan. "You are going to make us late!"

Toby stuck out his chin. "I am not going!"

Scott hurried to him and looked down at him. "Why, Toby?"

Toby shrugged and Vera walked to him and slipped her arms around him. "You've been looking forward to this party," she said. "Why have you changed your mind?"

Libby pushed her hands into her jacket pockets to

keep them warm as she waited for Toby's answer.

Finally he said, "I can't leave Goosy Poosy. Those boys are going to steal him and eat him for Christmas dinner!"

"What?" asked Vera in alarm. "What boys?"

"They were only teasing," said Kevin. "I heard them on the bus today and I know they were teasing."

"That's not a very nice way to tease," snapped Susan.

"They were not teasing!" Toby's face twitched and tears slipped down his cheeks. He turned and pushed his face against Vera's coat and she held him close.

Scott knelt beside Toby. "I'll be home, Toby. I'll watch so that no one takes Goosy Poosy. You can go to the party and have fun."

Libby smiled and wanted to tell Scott he was the very nicest person in the whole world.

Toby turned to look at Scott. "Will you really guard Goosy Poosy?"

Scott nodded and Toby sighed and said, "All right. I'll go to the party, but if anything happens, you call me at Connie Tol's house."

Scott grinned and nodded as he stood up. "I will. I promise. You won't have to worry about a thing."

"Can we go now?" asked Susan impatiently.

"Get into the car," said Vera.

Libby sat near the window with Susan beside her and Ben on the other side of Susan. Kevin and Toby sat in front with Vera. Libby waved at Scott and he waved back and her heart jumped a funny little jump.

Snow started falling again just as Vera turned onto the road toward town. Libby leaned back and watched the snow swirl around the car. Maybe they'd get snowed in and wouldn't have school tomorrow and she could stay home and be near Scott for the entire day. She smiled dreamily then stopped before Susan noticed.

Libby closed her eyes as she thought about the first time she'd gone to a party at Connie's house. Brenda Wilkens had hated her then, and Brenda had caused a lot of trouble. Brenda would be there tonight, but she was a friend now and not an enemy. Nobody would be there to make trouble tonight. Libby unzipped her jacket as the heater blew out too much hot air. Vera talked with Toby and Kevin as Libby thought about what she could tell Jill Noteboom about Scott. Jill always wanted to hear everything.

"Hear we are," said Vera as she stopped in front of a small white house. "I'll be back about nine to get you. Have a good time. Toby, don't worry about Goosy Poosy. You know Scott will take care of him."

Libby heard him say he couldn't help worrying anyway as she followed Susan to the door. Susan pressed the doorbell and almost immediately the door opened and Connie greeted them gaily. She had a spray of holly pinned to the collar of her blouse, and her dark hair was held back with bright red ribbons.

Jill Noteboom rushed forward and grabbed Libby's arm. "What kept you? I've been waiting forever!" She looked around, then back at Libby, her brows raised in question. She whispered, "Where is Scott Norris?"

Libby darted a look around her. "He said he was too old to come."

"I'm sorry, Libby." Jill shook her head and her curls bounced around her face. "I know you wanted him to be here."

Libby walked to the bedroom and flopped her jacket on the pile of coats. She turned and almost bumped into

Susan who was standing in front of the mirror, brushing her hair.

"Is Joe here yet, Jill?" asked Susan.

Jill nodded. "He's already in the basement."

Susan smiled and rushed out, leaving Jill and Libby alone in the bedroom. Jill laughed. "Remember how we made fun of Susan for being in love?"

Libby flushed. "I don't know if I'm in love, Jill. I just know I like Scott a lot."

Jill rolled her eyes. "And I like Adam a lot."

"Is he here yet?"

Jill nodded "He's downstairs. Shall we go down?" She grinned as she motioned toward the stair.

Libby walked ahead of Jill down the stairs to the noise of shouting and laughing. The room looked full. Libby searched for Adam and finally spotted him talking with Ben near the fireplace. Susan stood beside the piano, talking to Joe as if she hadn't seen him for days instead of just a few hours ago on the school bus. Libby leaned against the wall. If Scott had come, would he have stayed beside her and talked to her?

Jill nudged Libby. "Look who just walked in," she said in a very low voice.

Libby looked and her heart sank as Joanne Tripper stood at the bottom of the steps, looking very beautiful in a red blouse and pants.

"She thinks she's so gorgeous and so perfect," whispered Jill. "She doesn't have a weight problem like I do."

Libby bit the inside of her bottom lip as Joanne walked past and stopped beside Ben and Adam. She caught Adam's arm and laughed up at him.

Jill squeezed Libby's arm and Libby almost cried out

in pain. "She had better leave him alone," whispered Jill fiercely.

Libby felt like grabbing Joanne by the arm and tossing her outdoors in the snow. "Who invited her anyway? This is a church party and she sure doesn't go to church!"

Libby turned at a sound on the stairs. "April and May are here," she said excitedly. "They said before they probably couldn't come."

"I wish I could tell them apart," said Jill with a frown. "They both have long light brown hair and they are the same size and everything! And of course they are both gorgeous!"

Libby poked Jill's arm and laughed. "You look good, too, Jill."

"Not good, but better since I lost all that weight. But I will never be as beautiful as the Brakie twins."

"Hi, Libby. Hi, Jill," the twins said together.

"Hi, April. Hi, May," said Libby with a pleased smile. She knew which one was which and it was fun to watch others try to tell them apart. "I thought you were going away tonight."

April shrugged with a giggle. "We didn't. We wanted to come here. Did Scott come? I can't wait to meet him."

Libby forced back a blush. The twins must not know how she felt, but had they somehow guessed from her actions?

"He couldn't come," said Jill quickly. "But look who did show up."

May groaned. "How could anyone let Joanne Tripper in here? Oops, sorry. I promised that I would be very careful of what I say. I'm learning to love with Jesus' love."

Libby squirmed uncomfortably. She'd been learning

that also, but often she forgot. It was easy to love someone nice, but it was very hard to love a girl like Joanne Tripper.

Connie rang a small bell and called for attention. "We have planned games right now. Please choose a partner and we'll begin the first game."

Libby turned to grab Jill, but she was rushing toward Adam. Before Jill could reach Adam, Joanne Tripper had already picked him. Jill walked back, her head down, her face red.

"Don't worry about it," whispered Libby, feeling sorry for Jill. "You can have him for a partner in another game."

Libby joined in the games, but she wished that Scott was beside her, especially when Jill and Adam were partners and Libby was stuck with Toby. He seemed to be enjoying himself and that made her feel better.

After the games Connie stood at the piano, smiling as she looked at everyone sitting on the floor. "We have a special surprise for everyone tonight. We are going to hear a piano solo by an outstanding pianist."

Libby puffed with pride. She had not expected Connie to have her play for the group.

"Joanne Tripper came as my guest tonight, and she's agreed to play for us," said Connie with a proud smile at Joanne.

Libby wanted to sink through the floor, but she clapped with the others as Joanne walked to the piano and sat down.

Jill nudged Libby and made a face as Joanne played.

Libby locked her fingers together in her lap. Joanne could really play! Maybe someday Joanne Tripper would be a famous concert pianist and Elizabeth Gail Johnson would be an ugly nobody!

SEVEN
Scott's love

With a sigh Libby opened her locker door and pushed her books inside. Why couldn't her friends stop talking about Joanne's great piano playing? Why had Ben excitedly told Scott about it when they reached home last night? Now, Scott would be more impressed with Joanne than with her. Tears stung Libby's eyes and she blinked them back. She could not cry in the school hall for everyone to see!

"Hey, Libby."

Libby turned with a frown. "What do you want, Joanne?"

Joanne hugged her white, fur-trimmed coat against herself. "Why didn't you play last night, Libby? Were you afraid they'd all know that I really am better at piano than you?"

Libby doubled her fists at her sides. "Go home, Joanne. I'm just glad I won't have to see you for almost two weeks."

Joanne laughed mischievously. "Connie Tol invited me to play at your church sometime soon. I said I would."

Libby bit her lip and slammed her locker door closed with a bang. She jerked her jacket on as Joanne walked away laughing. Libby zipped her jacket and pulled on her hat, then rushed out of the school. She had to get onto the bus and sit in the back in a corner away from everyone! But she would not cry, at least not until she was home locked safely in her own bedroom.

Jill caught Libby's arm and Libby glared at her. Jill gasped and dropped her hand. "What's wrong, Libby? Are you mad at me?"

Libby pushed her way onto the bus and to the back. She sank down and slumped low in the seat. Jill dropped down beside her.

"Tell me, Libby."

Libby shook her head. How could she tell Jill that her plans to be a famous concert pianist might not happen? Maybe Jill already knew it by having heard Joanne Tripper last night.

"Is Goosy Poosy gone? Is that it?" asked Jill impatiently.

Libby shook her head, then sat up and turned to Jill. "But Scott said that someone had been sneaking around the chicken house and unlocked the gate before he could scare them away."

"Oh, my!"

"Toby didn't want to come to school today, but Scott said he'd guard the chickens and Goosy Poosy."

Jill shook her head. "This would make a very interesting book, wouldn't it? Maybe I should put away the one I'm working on and write this one. I wonder who would want to steal a goose?"

"Toby said that some boys want to eat Goosy Poosy for Christmas dinner." Libby made a face. "That's really disgusting!"

"We've had goose for Christmas dinner and I like it," said Jill, nodding.

Libby frowned. "But not Goosy Poosy! Who could eat a pet? I would like to get those boys and make them eat their words!"

Jill chuckled. "Libby, when you are fourteen, will you still be a fighter?"

Libby flushed and looked down at her jeans. Why should she fool herself? She'd never change. She couldn't be a Susan Johnson who acted like a lady. She couldn't be anything but what she was. "I didn't mean to embarrass you, Libby. I like you the way you are. Someday when we're both famous, we'll laugh about what we were like."

The bus stopped and several kids climbed off. Libby turned to say something to Jill, but she was looking at Adam with a dreamy expression, so Libby closed her mouth and turned to stare out the window. The snow piled alongside the road was already dirty.

The bus stopped again and Jill stood up. "I'll see you after a while, Libby."

Libby nodded as she remembered that they had made plans for that afternoon. Now, she wouldn't have time to cry in her room. Oh, well, she didn't much feel like it now.

A few minutes later Libby walked up the long drive toward the large house. Her heart raced. Was Scott watching for her out the window? Would he want to sit down with her and talk awhile?

Later she stopped in the family room door and peeked inside. Scott sat on the couch reading a book, his long legs crossed. He was dressed in faded jeans and a medium blue sweater shirt. Oh, but he was good looking! Would he mind if she walked in and interrupted his reading?

He looked up, then jumped to his feet. "How was school today, Elizabeth? I didn't hear you come in. Sit down and tell me about your day."

Slowly she walked in. Should she sit on the couch beside him or across from him in Chuck's chair? The log in the fireplace snapped and she jumped, then laughed self-consciously.

"Did you want to practice the piano right now instead?" asked Scott as he dropped his book on the end table.

She shook her head and licked her dry lips. "I would like to talk."

He smiled and sat down. "Let's talk."

She sank down on Chuck's chair and looked at him. What could she say to him? "It's cold out today."

He nodded. "I know. I went for a long hike this afternoon. I was glad for my heavy coat."

"Joanne Tripper plays the piano better than me." Why had she said that? Oh, my! She looked down at her stocking feet and wanted to fade into nothing.

"I talked to Joanne about her playing." Scott pushed his fingers through his dark hair. "She really is determined to be a concert pianist. I admire her. And I admire you, Elizabeth. You are doing what you want to do, and you spend a lot of time practicing so that you will do it well."

"I might not make it!" She knew she sounded as if she would burst into tears, but she couldn't help it.

"You'll make it, Elizabeth. Joanne has nothing to do with whether you make it or not. There are many concert pianists, but there is always room for another.

Maybe Joanne plays better at this time because she's taken lessons longer than you have. Don't compare yourself with her." Scott leaned forward earnestly. "You are a Christian, Elizabeth. God has given you your ability. You can be a great pianist because of that."

Libby jumped up and rushed to the couch. She sank down beside Scott and caught his hand in hers. "Do you believe that, Scott? Are you saying that just to make me feel good?"

He squeezed her hand and smiled. "I haven't known you long, Elizabeth, but I know that you will get what you want. You have determination. You can't fail."

Her eyes sparkled as she looked at his dear face. "Oh, Scott!"

"I'm glad I could say something to cheer you up. I hate to see you unhappy." He leaned forward and kissed her cheek. "You are special, Elizabeth Gail Johnson!"

She stared at him, her mouth hanging open, her hand on the kiss. He had kissed her! He thought she was special! Oh, he loved her! Dare she tell him that she loved him? What would he do?

Scott leaned back on the couch and crossed his legs. "Are you glad Christmas vacation finally started?"

She nodded. She could not speak yet.

"We'll have to do something fun together."

He did care! He wanted to be with her! Libby's heart raced. "We could go riding. Ben would let you ride Star and I'll ride Snowball."

"That sounds great! Maybe we could take a few sandwiches and have a winter picnic."

Libby felt as if she would burst with happiness. What would Jill say about this? Suddenly Libby jumped up. "Oh, I forgot! Jill is coming over and I have to change."

"See you later." Scott smiled as he reached for his book. He changed his mind and stood up. "I'd better find Toby and report to him. Today was uneventful in the life of Goosy Poosy." He laughed as he walked to the door with Libby. "See you later."

"Yes," she said softly. She watched him walk into the kitchen, then she raced upstairs to her room. She felt as if she were flying. Why didn't she keep a diary like Susan so that she could record every word that Scott had said?

Later Libby stood in the front yard with Jill. A pickup drove past and Rex barked. Libby laughed as she scooped up a handful of snow and threw it at a large maple.

"You look very happy, Libby. Your eyes are sparkling and you have roses in your cheeks," said Jill as she sat on the swing and twisted around to see Libby.

"I am happy. Scott loves me!" Oh, it sounded beautiful to say out loud!

Jill jumped up and grabbed Libby's arms. "How do you know? Tell me everything. How do you feel? How did he tell you?"

Libby pulled away and walked slowly toward the cow barn and Jill walked beside her. "He kissed me, Jill."

"He did? On the mouth? Oh, Libby!" Jill pressed her hand to her heart. "Oh, Libby!"

"He kissed me right here." She softly touched her cheek. "He said that I'm special."

"Oh, Libby!"

"He said we could go horseback riding together and have a winter picnic." Libby turned to Jill with stars in her eyes. "I know he must love me! And I love him!"

"You do?" whispered Jill breathlessly. "You never

would say that before, even when I knew you really did."

"I didn't know for sure, but now I do. I love Scott Norris!" Libby looked around quickly to make sure no one had heard, then stopped with a gasp. "Jill, there is someone sneaking around the chicken house again. Look!"

"I see him! Maybe he's the one trying to steal Goosy Poosy. Let's go get him!"

Libby dashed with Jill toward the chicken house. Should she call Scott to come help them? If she did, the spy would get away.

She stumbled on a stick in the snow and almost fell. Rex tugged against his chain and barked hard. He knew whoever was spying on them didn't belong.

"Where did he go?" asked Jill, gasping for breath as she stopped beside the tree near the chicken house.

"I saw him disappear in those trees," said Libby, pointing. She frowned thoughtfully. "Was he here to spy on us or to take Goosy Poosy?"

"He's gone now. Let's go tell the others," said Jill.

Libby hurried toward the house. Scott would know what to do. He knew practically everything.

EIGHT
The Johnsons' party

Libby waited near the back door as she looked longingly at the pond where Scott was already skating with a few early guests. If she were on the pond now, would Scott skate with her?

Finally the door opened and Vera handed a large tray of food to Libby. "Put this beside the paper plates on the picnic table, please. I can bring the rest of the stuff, so you stay there if you want to."

Libby smiled. "I'm glad we're having a party this afternoon. It'll be a lot of fun."

"Maybe it'll cheer Toby up. He hasn't been happy for several days now and I don't know why." Vera frowned and shook her head, then closed the door."

Libby hurried to the picnic table next to the pond. The bonfire that Ben had built earlier blazed high and hot. Kevin stood beside the table, pushing a potato chip into his mouth. He grinned sheepishly.

"I was hungry," he said.

Libby laughed as she unloaded the tray. "You are *always* hungry, Kevin."

He swallowed and wiped his hand across his mouth. "Where's Toby?"

Libby looked toward the ice with a thoughtful frown. "I thought he was out here already." She caught back a gasp. Scott was skating with Jill Noteboom! And they were laughing!

"What's wrong, Elizabeth?" asked Kevin, looking toward the ice.

"Did I say anything was wrong? I want to know where Toby is. His friends are here already. He should be out here with them." How could she watch her best friend with Scott? What would Jill say to Scott? She wouldn't dare tell him any secrets, would she?

Just then Vera walked up and set a tray of cupcakes on the table. "Is Toby on the ice yet, Kevin?"

"No, Mom. We don't know where he is."

"I'll look in the house," Libby said quickly. Maybe when she came back out, Scott would be skating alone.

What if he never asked her to skate with him?

Libby stood inside the porch door and leaned heavily against it. Had she been wrong yesterday about Scott's feelings toward her? Oh, she dare not think that! He had to love her!

She pushed herself away from the door and squared her shoulders. She must find Toby and get back outdoors.

The house smelled like pine from the Christmas tree. The silence was unusual as Libby looked from one room to another. She finally stopped at the bottom of the stairs and looked up. She did not want to hunt upstairs for him also.

"Toby!" she called loudly. "Mom wants you right now!" She waited, her hand on the bannister. "Toby!

You'd better get down here!" Was he upstairs? If he were, he'd have come by now. He knew the rule about coming when he was called.

Toby stopped at the top of the stairs and looked down at Libby. "What do you want?" he asked sharply.

"Why aren't you ready? The party's already started."

He stood with his doubled fists on his hips. "I don't want to go outdoors. I'm going to stay in and read or something."

Libby stamped her foot. "You have friends here, Toby. You have to come out with me. Now, get ready!"

"I don't have friends. They are Kevin's friends."

Libby caught the sadness in his voice and she sighed. "Cut it out, Toby. You know better than that."

He sniffed, then slowly walked down the steps. His red hair was mussed and his nose runny. Libby could tell he'd been crying and sucking his thumb.

"Blow your nose and let's go." She turned to leave, then turned back when he stayed on the steps.

"Well? Come on!" Was Scott still skating with Jill? Maybe he was looking for her. She scowled at Toby. "If you don't get your snowsuit on, I'm going to stuff you in it and drag you out."

Toby sniffed and rubbed the back of his hand across his nose. "I won't skate. I'll just stand there and freeze to death!"

"Oh, Toby." Libby caught his arm and pulled him to the back porch. "Get your coat on now!"

Giant tears welled up in his eyes and spilled out onto his cheeks.

Libby sagged against the door frame. What could she do to help Toby? Why wasn't Chuck home to help him?

Chuck would know what to do and say. "Why are you crying, Toby?" she asked sharply.

"I don't know." He sniffed harder.

"Yes, you do. Tell me what's wrong so we can get to the party before everyone goes home."

"Nobody loves me," he said in a low, hurt voice.

She didn't know whether to slap him or hug him. "Oh, Toby."

"I'm no good. I don't deserve to live here and be a Johnson. I should be sent back to Social Service so Mrs. Blevins can put me in a foster home where I'll get beaten and starved."

Libby shook her head. "Toby, Toby. What is wrong? Why do you feel this way?"

He looked up at her, his hazel eyes wide. "I let Max take money from Scott's dresser."

"You what? How could you, Toby? From Scott's room! Oh, dear!"

"See how bad I am?" Toby pressed his face against Chuck's farm coat and sobbed uncontrollably.

Libby hesitated, then slipped her arms around him and held him tightly, her head pressed against his. She could hear his heart beating and feel him trembling. "It's all right, Toby. We will explain to Scott and then get the money back from Max."

"But he spent it! I know he did! He wanted it for shopping this morning." His voice ended in a wail.

"How much was it, Toby?"

"Five dollars." Toby looked down at his bare feet.

"I'll take my money from my piggy bank and pay Scott back." Had she really offered to do that? Why had she done such a dumb thing? That money was to buy Scott something special for Christmas.

Toby knuckled away his tears. "Thanks, Libby. I wanted to use my money, but I don't have any left. I'll pay you back after Christmas. I promise!"

Libby nodded and sighed. "Get ready and let's get outside, Toby."

He barely smiled. "I'll get my socks and be right back." He ran down the hall and thudded up the stairs.

Libby stood at the window beside the back door and looked out. How many guests had arrived so far? At least Joanne Tripper would not be coming.

Libby watched three boys run across the yard. Why weren't they at the pond skating with the others or sledding on the hill? Libby shrugged. Those boys could take care of themselves. She would not worry about them. When she got outdoors, she'd find Scott and skate with him.

At the pond Toby ran off to skate with Robby Preston, and Libby slowly skated along the edge of the pond, looking for Scott. Had he stopped skating already? Maybe he was on the other side of the bonfire out of sight.

Susan skated past with Joe; then Jill and Adam followed. Where was Scott? Libby turned, then blushed hotly. He was just a short distance away watching her.

"I've been looking for you, Elizabeth."

He had? Oh! She slipped and almost fell. How could she be so clumsy in front of Scott? What must he think? "I was in the house getting Toby."

"Shall we skate?" He held out his hand with a smile. She held out her hand and felt like the most beautiful girl around as his hand closed over hers. He smiled and she did too as they skated around the pond.

"Jill told me she's writing a book," he said.

Jill? "Oh. Oh, yes, she is. She's been writing it since I first met her last year."

"I think it's wonderful. I spent the morning talking with her father. He's a very successful writer."

So that's where Scott had been all morning. She had tried to find him without seeming obvious. "I've read his books and liked them."

"I asked him if others thought he should go to a regular job instead of staying home to write." Scott tightened his hold on her hand and she looked at the intent expression on his face. "He said people used to feel that way, but now that he's well known, no one says anything."

"I know he works very hard." Why was Scott so interested in Ted Noteboom?

Scott nodded. "He said he works harder than when he worked in a small parts factory on the line. But he said he enjoys writing so much that he usually doesn't mind the long hours."

"Doctors work hard, too."

Scott sighed. "I know."

She looked at him thoughtfully. The brown scarf around his neck almost matched the color of his hair. "Scott, don't you want to be a doctor?"

He looked sharply at her. "Why do you ask?"

She shrugged. "I guess it was a dumb question."

He skated her around a group of boys. "I have never said this to another person, Elizabeth, but I really don't want to be a doctor."

He was sharing a secret with her? Her eyes sparkled and she wanted to turn to him and throw her arms around him instead of just skating along with her hand in his. "What do you want to do?" she asked breathlessly. Before he could answer, Ben shouted, "Someone's in the chicken house!"

"Goosy Poosy!" screamed Toby, scrambling to the edge of the pond. He jerked off his skates as fast as he could and pulled on his boots.

Libby's fingers felt all thumbs as she pulled off her skates. She glanced at Scott and he was already racing after Toby and Ben to the chicken house. Had someone stolen another chicken? Or had those boys really stolen Goosy Poosy so they could eat him for Christmas dinner?

Libby raced with the others to the chicken pen. Suddenly she remembered the three boys that she'd seen earlier running across the yard. Had those boys broken into the chicken house? Who were they?

Chickens ran squawking around the yard. Ben yelled, "Don't chase them! Let's get behind them so they'll run by themselves back into the pen."

Scott ran down the driveway, then came up behind several chickens. "Shoo," he said, waving his arms at them. They ran in their funny side-to-side run toward the barn and Kevin yelled at them and they ran the other way.

Toby dove after a large red hen and caught her by the leg. She squawked and he held her against himself until she quieted. Then he carried her to the pen and set her inside. He looked around and Libby saw the fear on his face.

"Goosy Poosy is gone!" Toby cried. "He's not in the pen or in the yard."

"Maybe he's inside the chicken house," said Joe. "I'll look."

In a few minutes Joe hurried back out. "He's not in there."

Susan ran to Joe and caught his hand. "Oh, Joe. We have to find Goosy Poosy."

Libby looked helplessly around the yard. Where was Goosy Poosy? Would the big white goose ever again walk around the Johnson farm and act like king of the yard?

NINE
Where is Goosy Poosy?

Libby's eyes filled with tears as she slowly walked to the chicken pen and looked through the wire. Where was Goosy Poosy? They had searched for him, and then finally Vera had said they'd have to eat so the guests could go home on time. Libby swallowed hard. The hot dog she'd forced down still seemed to be caught in her throat.

"We'll find Goosy Poosy, Elizabeth," said Scott as she turned to face him, tears sparkling in her eyes. "Don't cry."

"Maybe Susan is right and he is lying in a roaster with all his feathers off!" Libby clenched her hands in front of her. She heard Ben and Kevin near the barn, still looking for Goosy Poosy. The last guest had gone home. Jill had said to call her the minute they found Goosy Poosy. "Maybe we'll never see Goosy Poosy again!"

Scott pulled out a big hankie and wiped the tears from her face. "We'll find him. We won't give up looking until we do."

"Toby said Greg probably took him. Why don't we go to his house and see?" She wanted to rest her head on Scott's shoulder and cry for Goosy Poosy. "Toby might be right."

"Where does Greg live?" Scott pushed his gloves into his back pocket. A red hen clucked and scratched in the dirt. "We'll get Toby and see if he knows."

Libby smiled weakly. "Thanks, Scott."

He smiled and winked, then hurried away. Libby watched him talk to Ben and her legs felt suddenly very weak. Scott had wiped away her tears. He had told her his secret thoughts when they'd skated together. And he wanted to help find Goosy Poosy just as badly as the Johnsons!

Just then Toby rushed toward Libby, his face bright red. "I saw something move in those trees! Let's see if Greg and his brothers took Goosy Poosy up there."

Libby narrowed her eyes and tried to see in the trees on the hill, but she couldn't see anything.

"Let's go look," said Scott, leading the way.

Libby ran beside Toby across the field and up the hill. Maybe Toby had seen a deer or a dog. Why hadn't Rex barked from his doghouse? Toby had probably been imagining things.

Finally at the top of the hill, Libby gasped for breath and leaned weakly against a young oak. Was Goosy Poosy in the woods with Greg?

"Greg is sure going to be sorry when I see him again!" cried Toby, panting for breath. "If he hurt Goosy Poosy, I don't know what I'll do to him!"

Libby nodded as she pushed her hair out of her face. "I'll help you, Toby." She frowned. "But maybe Greg didn't take Goosy Poosy." Maybe Goosy Poosy would never be seen again, like the black and white chicken that had disappeared. What would they do if that happened? Her stomach cramped and she pressed her forehead against the tree. God cared about animals. He cared about Goosy Poosy. "Please, heavenly Father, help us find Goosy Poosy," she whispered through dry lips.

She lifted her head and heard the boys walking around and talking. Slowly she walked around a large oak and some underbrush that still had snow on it. Something moved and she looked again, her eyes wide. Goosy Poosy lay under the brush and he was tied up! "Scott! Ben! Kevin and Toby! Come quick!" She jumped up and down and pointed down at the big goose that blended in with the snow.

Scott reached her first, and he immediately knelt in the snow and untied Goosy Poosy. "Are you hurt? Can you walk all right?"

"Goosy Poosy!" cried Toby and Kevin together as Toby dropped down beside the goose and wrapped his arms around him. "Oh, are you all right?" Toby's voice sounded full of tears.

Libby looked thankfully at Scott who was smiling down at Toby.

"Let's get him back to the pen," said Ben, tugging his hat lower over his ears. "Then we have to get the chores done before it gets too dark."

Goosy Poosy swayed back and forth as he walked beside Toby down the hill. Libby hung back and made sure she was beside Scott. She wanted to walk with him and talk with him again.

"I wonder if we'll ever know who did that to Goosy Poosy," said Scott in a low voice.

"We'll find out," said Libby firmly. "We sure will find

out!" She walked beside Scott to the yard and stood watching Kevin open the gate to the chicken pen.

"Wait a minute," said Scott. "Maybe we should put Goosy Poosy in the barn for the night."

"That's a good idea," said Ben, nodding. "We can put him in a stall in the horse barn. No one would think to look for him there."

Toby hugged the goose tightly as he stared at Ben with wide eyes. "Do you think someone will try to take him again? I'd better sleep in the barn with him!"

"Mom won't let you," said Kevin, shaking his head.

"I'll sneak out!" Toby rubbed his cheek against Goosy Poosy's neck.

Libby looked helplessly at Scott. He smiled reassuringly as he squeezed Toby's shoulder.

"Let's take him to the barn and feed and water him," said Scott. "He's probably tired and sleepy after his adventure."

Toby walked the goose to the horse barn. Snowball and Apache Girl nickered and Libby told them she'd feed them in a minute. "You will have a guest tonight, Snowball." Libby rubbed her white filly. "Goosy Poosy is spending the night. Aren't you pleased?"

Scott laughed. "Does she understand you, Elizabeth?"

"Of course." Libby flushed but smiled.

"Goosy Poosy likes it in here," said Kevin as he looked over the stall door. "I think he wants to have this be his home from now on. He thinks he's too good to stay in with the chickens."

"I'm staying in here with him," said Toby in a loud, determined voice.

Scott walked to Toby. "You won't have to, Toby. I'll check on Goosy Poosy before I go to bed tonight, and I'll sleep with one eye and ear open. We'll let Rex run loose tonight and if anyone comes around, he'll bark up a storm."

Toby looked uncertain, then finally agreed. "But I'm going to get up early tomorrow and come out here to see about him!"

"Me, too," said Kevin, nodding his head.

"Let's do the chores," said Ben as he walked toward the door.

Libby watched them walk out; then she opened the grain barrel and scooped out grain. A gray barn cat rubbed against her ankle and she bent to pet him. He purred loudly and Libby laughed.

Libby worked quickly and just as she finished, the door opened and Scott walked in. Her heart almost leaped through her jacket.

"I thought you might need help," he said with a smile. "I helped Ben all I could; then I fed and watered the sheep."

"You did? Thank you." My, but it was hard to breathe with Scott beside her!

"Susan was very glad to know Goosy Poosy was back safe. Vera was, too. She called Chuck to tell him." Scott picked up the barn cat and held him close. The cat purred and Scott laughed.

"I'm finished already, but thanks anyway, Scott." She just stood there looking at him and didn't want to move.

Scott walked to the door and held it open for her. She slowly walked outdoors where it was already getting dark. What would it feel like if Scott kissed her the way Joe kissed Susan? Her face blazed and she turned it quickly away before Scott noticed.

He stopped her just outside the back door of the house. She looked up at him questioningly.

"Elizabeth, I didn't mean to tell you that I don't want to be a doctor. Please don't tell anyone else. I don't want my parents to know how I feel. They are counting on their only son to do something really worthwhile."

Tears pricked her eyes and she wanted to do something to comfort him. "I won't say anything." She looked down at her boots, then up into his face. "Scott, I'm sorry that you aren't happy. I want you to be happy."

He smiled. "Thanks for caring."

"Oh, I do!" If only he knew how much!

"Play for me, Elizabeth Gail Johnson. I want to hear the soft notes of the piano right now." He reached around her and opened the back door. She walked in and pulled off her coat and boots. She'd play for him and she'd cheer him up.

He stood his boots beside Chuck's, then pushed his fingers through his dark hair. "I really don't want to be a doctor, Elizabeth. I'm afraid it'll start to show up in my grades, and then my parents will really be disappointed. I wish I knew what to do."

Smells of roast beef drifted onto the back porch. Christmas music filled the air. Libby caught Scott's hand and tugged him toward the family room. "I'll cheer you up, Scott. I promise."

He squeezed her hand. "For some reason, Elizabeth, you usually do."

She gently pushed him down on Chuck's chair; then she sat at the piano. What would he do if she told him she loved him? She fumbled with the music book and it fell to the floor. He jumped up to pick it up just as she bent down. Her head cracked against his and she cried out with pain, gingerly rubbing the spot. Tears sprang

76

to her eyes and she tried to blink them away before Scott saw them, but she was too late.

"I'm sorry, Elizabeth." He moved her hand and gently touched the spot. "You have a little lump there, but it'll go away. I am very sorry."

She smiled. "Don't worry about it." She could feel his warm breath on her cheek.

He helped her up and led her to Vera's chair. "You sit there and relax awhile and I'll play for you."

"Can you play?" she asked in surprise as he pulled out the bench, then sat down.

He shrugged, then ran his fingers up and down the keys. He looked over his shoulder at her, then smiled. "I play my own style."

"It's beautiful!"

He leaned forward over the piano and sang along with his playing in a pleasant tenor voice. Libby had not heard the song before. It was full of praise and worship to God, and tears filled her eyes at the beauty of it.

Finally Scott turned to her, a strange look on his face. "What did you think of it?"

"I love the way you play!"

"No, I mean the song." He walked to the couch and sat on the edge.

"I loved the song and the playing and the singing! Sing it again."

He sat back and crossed his legs, his right ankle on his left knee. He locked his fingers behind his head and his elbows poked the air. "I wrote it."

Libby gasped. "You did? It's beautiful!"

"I sold the words and music. The company wants more from me."

"Then give them more!" Libby locked her fingers

together and leaned forward eagerly.

He pushed himself up and frowned. "I wish it was that simple. I wish it was."

She frowned up at him. "You have a dream, Scott. Why can't you work at it and make it happen?"

Scott stood with his back to the fireplace. "My dream. My parents' dream. My sister's dream. What dream should I fulfill? Whatever I do, I'll hurt someone."

Libby walked to him and slipped her arms around him. "I am sorry, Scott. I don't want you to feel bad. I love you. I want you to be happy."

A strange look crossed his face and he abruptly pushed her away. "I'd better go see if Chuck is home yet. I told him I'd help him with his bookwork tonight."

Libby's whole body felt hot with embarrassment as he hurried away. Why had she told him she loved him? Oh, she could never, never look at him again!

TEN
Day before Christmas

Libby pressed her head against Snowball's neck. She smelled dusty and Libby almost sneezed. "I don't know why I told Scott that I love him," she whispered miserably. "Now, he won't look at me or talk to me. I don't know what I'm going to do!"

Snowball nickered and moved her head. Her white winter hair was long and thick.

Goosy Poosy honked and Libby quickly led Snowball to the back door of the barn and let her out in the pen. "I'm coming, Goosy Poosy." How could life go on when she felt so terrible! She opened the stall door, and the big white goose half walked and half flew into the aisle. He honked with his long neck out. Libby quickly opened the front door of the barn and let him out. He spread his wings and ran across the yard. Libby hesitated with a thoughtful frown. Should she have kept Goosy Poosy locked in for the day? Would someone try to steal him again with everyone home? She shrugged, then closed the door, and walked back to feed Jack and Dan.

Libby stifled a yawn and her steps dragged as she

walked to Apache Girl's stall. The barn door opened and Libby jumped back, her face white, her hands trembling. It just could not be Scott! When she saw Ben, she took a long, shaky breath and the color rushed to her face.

"I brought Star a 'day before Christmas' treat," said Ben, grinning as he pulled an apple out of his pocket.

"She'll like that," said Libby. Did Ben know she loved Scott?

"I noticed that you let Goosy Poosy out." Ben stood beside Star's stall. "I hope nobody tries to take him today. I wonder if Greg did do it yesterday."

"We should think of a way to find out." Libby walked to Ben. "Let's plan a way to trap Greg, shall we?"

Ben hesitated, then nodded and grinned mischievously. "I'll get Toby to call him."

"We'll decide what Toby should say to Greg."

"Scott will know," said Ben.

Libby turned quickly away, her head down. "You ask him while I finish my chores."

Ben looked around questioningly. "Isn't Scott in here? I heard him say he wanted to talk to you."

Libby felt almost too weak to stand. "He didn't come in here."

"Maybe he thought you were taking care of the calves."

Libby looked around frantically for a place to hide in case Scott did come in the barn looking for her. What would he say to her?

"I thought you were going to town today to do a little more Christmas shopping, Elizabeth," said Ben over his shoulder as he walked toward the door.

"I didn't have to go after all." She could not buy Scott

something special now. Oh, why had she told him how she felt?

Ben opened the barn door and a gust of cold wind blew in. "Oh, hi, Scott. We were just talking about you."

Libby looked frantically around for a place to hide.

"I hope it was nothing bad," said Scott with a short laugh. He walked into the barn and Ben said he'd see them later.

Libby stood rooted to the spot, her face hot with embarrassment. How could she face Scott? But she couldn't hide now that he'd seen her. She stood with her shoulders back and her chin high. "Good morning," she said in a voice that sounded very natural. Could he hear her heart racing or see that her legs were trembling?

He twisted his gloves nervously. "Hi." He hesitated and she just stood quietly looking at him. "I saw Goosy Poosy."

She nodded.

"At least he made it through the night."

Libby nodded stiffly.

Scott pushed his fingers through his hair. "Elizabeth, I am sorry for misunderstanding you yesterday. I've put a barrier between us and I'm sorry. How could I have thought you meant you loved me as a boyfriend? You meant that you loved me as one person loves another who is hurting. I shared my feelings with you and you wanted to comfort me. I know that's all it was."

Libby's mind seemed to be spinning, but she managed a smile. "That's right, Scott." How could she stand in front of him and lie?

She could see the relief on his face and she was glad that she'd lied to him. How could the lie hurt? God wouldn't care, would he?

"Shall I help you finish in here?" Scott swung his hand in an arc.

"I'm finished already." She walked toward the door, suddenly needing fresh air.

The sun shone weakly and the sky was gray. Rex barked from his doghouse, straining against his chain.

Goosy Poosy squawked a strange squawk and Libby's head shot up. She saw someone running across the field with Goosy Poosy in his arms.

"Scott! Look!" Libby pointed with one hand as she grabbed Scott's arm with the other.

"Let's go." Scott raced across the yard toward the field behind the cow barn. Libby looked wildly around for Ben, but he wasn't in sight and she knew if she hunted him down, she'd never be able to catch up to Scott.

She raced across the yard, slipping once in the snow, then sped on. Scott was still a little way from the person carrying Goosy Poosy. Would Scott catch him and get their pet back? Libby's heart pounded with fear and her breathing was ragged as she ran. She reached the trees, then stopped uncertainly. Where was Scott and where was the person who had taken Goosy Poosy?

Oh, why had she let Goosy Poosy out of the barn? This time maybe the thief would kill Goosy Poosy for Christmas dinner! Was Greg the thief? Libby frowned thoughtfully. The thief looked bigger than Greg.

Where was Scott?

Libby strained her ears to hear him, but all she could hear was the distant bark of Rex and her own thudding heart.

Should she call to Scott? She wrapped her arms around herself and tried to stop shivering. She could not stand here all day. Where should she go? She would not go back to the farmyard without Scott. What if he got lost and wandered onto state property and never got out?

Oh, she should have told Scott the truth! She should have told him that she loved him as a boyfriend, just as Susan loved Joe and Jill loved Adam! Tears pricked her eyes and she blinked quickly. Would she ever have a chance to tell Scott? Would she grow old with that lie hanging over her?

"I can't stand here all morning," she muttered impatiently. She tugged her hat lower and looked around, then hurried through the trees. She remembered the time she and Susan had walked back here and been separated. She had gotten lost and Susan had stumbled against a root and fallen. She'd hurt her ankle and her head. Would that happen to Scott?

A noise to her left startled her and she stopped, her hand over her racing heart, her eyes wide.

Suddenly Scott walked from around a clump of birch and stopped when he saw Libby. His face was red and a twig was caught in his hair. "I lost the thief, Elizabeth. Whoever he was, he knows these woods and he knew how to get away from me."

"I thought you were lost," she said in a shaky voice.

"I'm all right, just embarrassed that I lost the thief." He pulled the twig from his hair and dropped it. "Toby will be very upset if we go back without Goosy Poosy. The whole family will be upset."

Libby caught his hand and looked up at him. "We won't give up! We'll find Goosy Poosy!"

Scott looked at her and his blue eyes were bright. "You never give up, do you?"

"I try not to."

He smiled and she did too. "Let's go find Goosy Poosy." He gripped her hand and she walked beside him through the woods.

ELEVEN
House in the woods

Libby watched nervously as Scott climbed the woven
wire fence that separated Johnson Property from
VanderWeele property. She reached out her hand, but
he held awkwardly to the fence post. She had easily
climbed over since she was light and agile. The fence
groaned under his weight. Suddenly his toe caught and
he sprawled headlong at Libby's feet.

"Scott!" She dropped beside him in the patchy snow
and cradled his head in her arms. "Are you hurt?"

He groaned and carefully pushed himself to a sitting
position. "Only my pride."

"I would die if anything happened to you!" Libby
caught his hand and hugged it to her. "Maybe we should
go home."

He tugged gently at his hand, but she wouldn't
release it. "I'm all right, Elizabeth. Let me up."

She flushed and immediately dropped his arm. She
jumped up, her heart thudding. Why had she acted that
way? Wouldn't she ever learn?

He groaned again as he stood up. He pressed his

hands to the small of his back. "Shall we try again? We don't want to give the thief enough time to pluck our goose." Scott chuckled and made a face. "I really am all right, Elizabeth. Are you sure you are?"

She ducked her head. "I just want to get Goosy Poosy and get him home." And she wanted to hide from Scott until she could think of what to do about him and the way she felt.

He cupped her chin in his hand and tipped her head up. "Did I hurt you again, Elizabeth?"

Her eyes filled with tears and she stood very still.

"I am sorry. I don't want to hurt you. You are important to me."

Her stomach tightened. "Scott, I *do* love you. I really love you and I'm sorry if you don't want me to, but I have to tell the truth."

He stepped back, his hand falling to his side. "I don't know what to say. This has never happened to me before."

Why couldn't he pull her close and say that he loved her too, and that he always would?

"Don't look at me that way. Don't cry, please!"

"I won't!" She knuckled away her tears and squared her shoulders. "Let's find Goosy Poosy."

He shook his head, then shrugged. "That's why we're here. Let's go."

She walked beside him, not looking at him. She'd told him, and she was not sorry!

After several minutes Scott stopped and she did, too. "Look," he whispered, pointing through the trees.

"A house with smoke coming from the chimney. Someone lives there!" exclaimed Libby.

Scott frowned as he reached for Libby's hand. "Stay

with me and we'll go to the door. Someone here might have seen Goosy Poosy."

Libby looked at his hand holding hers again and she wanted to press it against her cheek. How could she think about that when Goosy Poosy was still in danger? She looked apprehensively at the run-down, weathered gray house. Who lived there?

"Careful of the first step," said Scott as he carefully stepped to the next one.

Libby stepped over the broken step, then waited beside Scott as he lifted his hand to knock.

Just then someone spoke from beside the house, and Libby turned to find Carrie Brown.

"What are you doing here, Libby?" asked Carrie sharply. Her ragged coat hung open, and her jeans and shirt were worn thin and dirty. She didn't have on a hat or boots.

"Do you live here, Carrie?" asked Libby in surprise.

"What's it to you? Sure, we live here. Didn't Max tell you when he came to your house the other day?"

"Where is your brother?" asked Scott as he carefully walked down the steps.

"What brother? I got four of them." Carrie stood with her fists on her hips and her feet apart. Her braids were coming loose and wisps of hair hung around her pale face.

Libby looked around the unkempt yard to the weathered gray shed with a pile of wood beside it.

"Could we get a drink before we leave?" asked Scott.

Carrie hesitated, then nodded. "Then you get off our place." Carrie went into the house and returned with two glasses of water.

Libby glanced questioningly at Scott. Was he really thirsty or did he suspect Carrie and Max? Her mouth suddenly felt very dry, and the sight of the water made her realize how thirsty she really was.

The cold water felt good going down her throat. It dripped off her chin and she wiped it away with the back of her hand.

Just then the door to the house opened and several kids walked out. The door stood open and a small girl in diapers stepped out.

"Jane!" cried Carrie, dashing to her. "You get right back in the house! You will freeze out here!" Carrie lifted Jane and stood her inside, then slammed the door. Jane howled, but Carrie ignored her and frowned at Libby and Scott. "You got your drinks. Now get out of here."

"We're going," said Scott, but he didn't move.

Carrie grabbed one of the boys by the arm and shook him. "Al, you hear that baby crying? Why didn't you stay in there with her? It's your turn to watch her."

Al jerked away from Carrie and made a face at her. "You think you're so big!"

"I'm the boss here while Momma and Daddy are gone, and don't you forget it!" Carrie scowled at Al, and he backed away.

"Hi, Max," said Scott with a nod. "I haven't seen you since you were at the Johnsons'."

Libby bit her tongue to keep from telling him to give back the money he'd stolen from Scott.

"I been around," Max said, lifting his shoulder. "What's Toby doing today?"

"Getting ready for Christmas," said Scott. "Are you ready for Christmas?"

"We got a goose!" exclaimed one of the small boys

with a wide grin. "Carrie brought it home for our Christmas dinner."

Libby's stomach tightened as she looked quickly at Carrie. Carrie's face turned red and she frowned at the boy.

"Keep your mouth shut, Billy," she said gruffly. "Who cares if we got a goose?"

"I care," said Billy. "I like that goose." He grinned at Scott. "You want to see our goose?"

"Sure," said Scott.

"If you see one goose, you've seen them all," said Carrie. "What do you want to see an old brown goose for?"

"He ain't . . ." Billy stopped as Max grabbed his arm and twisted it sharply. "Let me go, Max! I ain't gonna say nothing. I just want to tell them our goose ain't their goose."

"Course he ain't their goose," snapped another boy who had the same dirty brown hair, the same ragged clothes.

Libby saw the looks pass between the kids and she turned toward the shed, her chin lifted in determination. She would see that brown goose for herself! She stepped toward the shed, but Carrie jumped in front of her and blocked her.

"Where do you think you're going, Libby Johnson?" asked Carrie angrily.

"To the shed, Carrie Brown! I don't trust a girl who takes candy from someone who wants to be a friend."

Carrie flushed, but didn't move.

"I want to see the goose, too," said Scott firmly. He took one step, but Max and two little boys jumped in the way.

"No," said Max, his eyes narrowed. "You can't!"

"Get away from here right now," demanded Carrie,

her fists doubled. "Go home where you belong to that red and pink bedroom and the magic puzzle box and everything. We sure didn't invite you to come here. We don't have a dozen bedrooms and a basement with a Ping-Pong table. We don't have nothing!"

Libby felt sorry for Carrie for a minute, then pushed the feeling away. "I am going to look at that goose!"

The baby in the house screamed loud and hard, and Carrie looked toward the house, then back at Libby, then at her brother. "Al, go see about Jane."

"Let Fred check on her," said Al. "I'm helping Max."

"So am I," said Fred gruffly.

Carrie stamped her foot. "Al! Get to the house before I bust you good!"

Al swore and Libby looked quickly at Scott. Had he ever heard that kind of talking?

Al dashed to the house and Libby leaped around Carrie toward the shed. Carrie grabbed Libby's arm and spun her around, then knocked her to the ground.

Libby leaped up, but once again Carrie was between her and the shed. "Get out of my way, Carrie! I mean it!"

Carrie pushed her face close to Libby. "You want me to break those long piano fingers?"

Libby's face paled and she stepped back a pace. "You're just talking big. You wouldn't do that to me or to anyone."

Carrie shrugged, but Libby didn't move again. "I won't let you get to that shed, Libby. You and this guy go back where you belong."

Libby glanced at Scott and he looked at her. She knew he was trying to decide what to do. He could handle Max, but with the two little boys with Max, he might not be able to do it without hurting someone.

How could she get to the shed to see if Goosy Poosy was inside? Wait a minute! She could find out if it was Goosy Poosy without seeing him. "Goosy Poosy!" she called loudly. "Goosy Poosy!"

Suddenly the goose honked and Libby could hear flapping sounds, the same flapping sounds Goosy Poosy made when he wanted out of the chicken house.

"Goosy Poosy!" she called again.

He honked again and she knew it was Goosy Poosy. "You turn our goose loose, Carrie Brown!" cried Libby.

"I'll call the police if you don't get out of here!" cried Carrie, her face red.

"You go right ahead and call them, and we'll prove who's goose you have," snapped Libby.

Scott suddenly jumped away from the boys and ran

toward the shed. Before he could reach it, Max stood at the shed door, an axe in his hands.

"Don't come no closer!" said Max, his face dark with rage.

Carrie and the little boys ran to stand beside Max, their faces set. "That goose is our Christmas dinner, and nobody is gonna take our Christmas dinner away from us!"

Libby looked at Scott. He stepped close to her and slipped his arm around her shoulders. Did he think this was the end of Goosy Poosy?

TWELVE
Home again

Libby pulled off her hat and let the cold wind blow against her damp hair. She scowled at Carrie and her brothers and tried to think of a way to get past them into the shed to set Goosy Poosy free.

Goosy Poosy honked wildly and beat against the closed door. Libby knew he wanted out as badly as she and Scott wanted to let him out. It was too bad that Kevin and Toby had not taught Goosy Poosy how to unlock a door.

"Just go home, Libby," said Carrie impatiently. "We don't want you here."

"I'm not going home without Goosy Poosy," said Libby, doubling her fists at her sides.

Scott stepped forward and Max held the axe higher. Libby swallowed hard and wanted to grab Scott and pull him back.

"You won't use that axe on us, Max," said Scott in a gentle voice. "You don't want to hurt anyone. Put the axe down and open the door for Goosy Poosy."

"Don't be dumb, mister," said Max with his eyes

narrowed. "We're keeping that goose."

"I don't think so," said Scott.

Libby held her breath as Scott stepped closer and closer to Max. What if Max hurt Scott, or even killed him? Libby's stomach tightened into a hard knot and fear pricked her skin. She could not live if anything happened to Scott Norris!

"Drop that axe, Max!" Scott's voice was full of authority and Libby knew if she were Max, she would obey. "You know that goose doesn't really belong to you. Don't make anything worse that it is already."

"Get off our place!" screamed Carrie, her face a brick red, her arms waving frantically. "That is our goose! You're rich and you can buy anything you want for Christmas dinner!"

Libby stepped beside Scott. "Carrie, Toby and Kevin and all our family love Goosy Poosy. He is a pet. He is not to eat for Christmas dinner! Goosy Poosy rides on Kevin's sled when he goes sledding. He eats out of Toby's hand. Toby would share his room with Goosy Poosy if Mom would let him. They've had Goosy Poosy since he was one day old and just a ball of yellow fluff. He thinks he's a person! He is not a Christmas dinner! He's part of the Johnson family!"

"Let's let him out," said Fred in a small, scared voice.

"Please," said Libby with her hands clasped in front of her. She saw Carrie hesitate and she watched Max lower the axe a little.

Scott stepped forward and lifted the axe from Max's hands. "You won't be sorry, Max."

Billy lifted the latch and pushed the door in. Goosy Poosy rushed out, honking indignantly. He flapped his wings, then ran in a circle.

94

"Now we won't have no Christmas dinner," said Fred sadly.

"You ruined everything!" cried Carrie, glaring at Libby. "You got what you wanted, now get away from here right now!"

Libby looked helplessly at the ragged kids, then turned to Scott. How could they help Carrie and her family? Libby turned away abruptly. What was she thinking? They didn't deserve any help. They should starve! They should have a terrible Christmas!

"Let's go, Elizabeth," said Scott.

Libby called to Goosy Poosy, then turned away from the sad-faced children. What could she do anyway? It wasn't her place to help them. She'd get Goosy Poosy home where he belonged and get ready for Christmas when Grandma and Grandpa Johnson would be coming for the day.

Libby walked out of the yard with Scott on one side of her and Goosy Poosy on the other. Libby's shoulders drooped and she fought against the tears that pricked her eyes. Why should she feel badly? Goosy Poosy was free and they were on their way home!

Scott stopped at the woven wire fence and picked up Goosy Poosy and dropped him over it. "This time I won't fall all over myself," he said with a chuckle.

Libby scrambled over and then watched Scott. "Did you know Goosy Poosy was locked in that shed?" she asked.

He grinned with a shrug. "I saw some white feathers that looked very suspicious. I didn't want to leave there until I knew that those feathers weren't Goosy Poosy's."

Libby stepped closer and looked up into his face. "You were very brave."

"Thanks. You were, too." Scott rubbed Goosy Poosy's neck. "And so were you, white goose. You have had quite an adventure. Now, it's time to get you home so you can enjoy the rest of the day."

Libby walked slowly along beside Scott. She wanted him to forget about Goosy Poosy for now and talk to her. She wanted him to say that he was glad that she loved him and that he loved her also. Why didn't he stop talking about how glad the boys would be to see their goose?

At the edge of the woods Scott stopped and turned to face Libby. She waited, her face lifted, her eyes sparkling.

"Elizabeth, I think we should take food to that family so they will have something for Christmas dinner."

She wanted to be angry that he didn't say he loved her, but she was so proud of him for feeling that way that she could only smile. "I think we should, too."

"Does your family have to know all the details about our adventure today?" asked Scott softly.

Libby hesitated, then smiled. "No, they don't. And I'm sure Mom will want to help make this Christmas a happy one for the Browns."

"You are special, Elizabeth."

"So are you, Scott." She smiled into his eyes and he smiled in a way that sent her pulse racing. He must love her a little! Finally he turned and walked down the hill and Goosy Poosy honked and swayed along with him.

Suddenly Libby couldn't just walk. She raced past Scott and sped down the hill toward the yard. She yelled, "Ben! Toby! Kevin! We have Goosy Poosy!"

In the yard the boys rushed to meet them and the back door slammed and Vera and Susan rushed out.

Toby dropped in the snow beside Goosy Poosy and

96

hugged him tightly and kissed his head. "I knew you'd come back. We prayed for you. I knew you'd be safe."

"Where was he?" asked Vera, pulling her coat closer.

Libby looked at Scott, then smiled at Vera. "We found him with Carrie Brown and her brothers."

Scott pushed his fingers through his dark hair. "Vera, that family needs something for Christmas dinner. Do you have anything that we could take to them?"

"We'll look in the freezer and the cupboard," she said as she turned toward the house. She looked over her shoulder. "Toby and Kevin, put Goosy Poosy in the horse barn again."

"I don't think anyone will try to take him again," said Scott.

"Toby called Greg," said Ben grimly. "Greg said he'd taken Goosy Poosy yesterday, but he said he hadn't today. I don't think Greg or his brothers will make any more trouble."

"Goosy Poosy, you are safe," said Toby as the goose rubbed his neck up and down Toby's arm.

Libby looked at Scott and smiled.

THIRTEEN
Christmas love

Libby smiled at Scott as he drove slowly down the rutted road leading back to the house in the woods. "Won't they be surprised?"

Scott nodded and chuckled. "At least they'll know what Christmas love is all about."

Libby nodded. Once she'd thought the Johnsons were very strange people. Now she knew that they were full of God's love and compassion for others. Chuck had told her often that God's love was inside her, too, and she smiled happily, knowing it was true.

"I don't know how people can live that way," said Scott as he stopped outside the small house. Smoke curled from the chimney and drifted up into the cold gray sky.

Libby bit the inside of her bottom lip as she reached to open the car door. Living in that house was much better than living in a bus station doorway or in a foster home full of hate. Scott probably didn't know about that kind of life.

The front door of the house opened and a short, wiry

man walked to the car. Scott met him near the hood. "You folks lost?" He rubbed his hand across the stubble on his jaw. "We get about two cars here a week with folks who missed the turn."

"We aren't lost, Mr. Brown," said Scott. He held out his hand "I'm Scott Norris. I'm visiting the Johnson family for Christmas." He motioned to Libby. "This is Elizabeth Johnson. She goes to school with Carrie."

The man nodded with a question in his eye as Libby said hello. "What can I do for you?" He looked from Libby to Scott.

Scott smiled. "Not a thing, sir. We want to do something for you. We want you to know that God loves you and your family. He laid it on our hearts to share some things with you this Christmas season."

Tears filled the man's eyes. "You don't say."

"I'll need your help to unload," said Scott. He walked to the back of the station wagon with Mr. Brown beside him. Libby lifted out a bag of fruit, then stepped aside as Scott handed Mr. Brown a large frozen turkey.

"Can this be?" he asked, shaking his head. "Me and Agnes just came back from town with only a little bit of food. She said God would provide, but I just laughed and said he who helps himself gets helped the quickest."

Libby followed Scott into the house. She saw the startled look on Carrie's face before she turned. She gasped. Standing in the corner was a blue spruce decorated with bows and garlands. She knew it was the tree that had been cut down from Ben's stand of Christmas trees. She once again looked at Carrie and she flushed and looked down at her feet.

Scott lifted the bag of fruit from Libby's arms and handed it to Max.

"This is just too much," said Mrs. Brown, wiping her eyes with the back of her hand.

"There's more in the car," said Scott.

"You don't say!" Mr. Brown rubbed his hand across his face and shook his head. "You was right, Momma. God did provide, and he sure did it up big!"

Libby swallowed the lump in her throat as she started for the door again.

"I'll help you," said Carrie quickly.

Libby walked into the cold air with Carrie beside her. The house had seemed close and hot.

"Libby, thanks for not telling on us about the goose," said Carrie under her breath.

Libby shrugged. "I'm learning to forgive people. Sometimes I forget, but I'm trying."

Carrie bit her lip. "Libby, I know you know about the tree. I'll pay Ben for it when I can. I promise."

"All right. You settle it with him, Carrie." Libby lifted a bag out and handed it to Carrie, then picked up the last one herself. "We do want you to have a merry Christmas, Carrie."

"We will now." Carrie laid her hand on Libby's arm. "I'm sorry for spying on you at your house." Carrie walked into the house and Libby followed, glad the mystery of the spy was solved. She knew Carrie wouldn't do it again.

Baby Jane toddled to Libby and tugged at her sleeve. "Cookie? Cookie?"

Libby smiled at the dirty-faced little girl. "We brought you a cookie, Jane."

Later Libby sat in the car as Scott drove back down the rutty road. She remembered all the Christmases when she'd been sad and lonely without even a Christmas cookie to cheer her up. This would be her third Christmas in the Johnson house, and it would be her third happy Christmas. She smiled at Scott. "I'm glad we could help them."

He nodded. "I don't know how I can feel sorry for myself after seeing that poor family. They don't have enough to eat or wear. I have all I need and want. I should be happy."

Libby twisted in the seat to face him. "Scott, how can you be happy if you try to make someone else's dream your dream? How can you be happy if you are going to be a doctor because your family wants that for you? You have to make your own dream come true."

He turned onto the main road and increased his speed. "It is not for you to say, Elizabeth," he said harshly.

"I want you to be happy, Scott! I love you!"

He frowned at her. "Did I ask you to? Did I ask you to love me? Did I ask you to butt in on my life?"

She turned away and stared through the windshield at the paved road. She locked her fingers together so tightly they hurt. Her heart seemed frozen inside her breast and her throat felt tight. How could he talk that way to her? Why had she said anything to him? The day had been so wonderful and now it was completely ruined.

He stopped outside their garage and she jumped from the car and ran to the house. Tears spilled down her cheeks as she jammed her jacket on the hook. Christmas was ruined. Her life was ruined. She would never be happy again as long as she lived!

FOURTEEN
Scott Norris

Libby walked listlessly to the horse barn. How could Christmas day be so dreary and cold?

Just then Susan called to her and Libby forced a bright smile and turned. Susan's cheeks were flushed with bright color and her blue eyes sparkled brightly. "Just as soon as I finish chores, Joe is coming over with my Christmas gift. I can't wait to see what he got me!"

"You'd like it even if it was a stick tied with a string," said Libby, forcing a laugh. How long could she keep up this happy face? Last night and this morning opening gifts she'd forced herself to smile and talk happily. Maybe later when Jill came over she could tell her everything and cry if she wanted to.

"Thanks again for the Don Francisco tape," said Susan. "I like his songs."

"Me, too." Would gospel singers someday sing Scott Norris's songs? Or would he forget that part of his life and continue to study medicine? Why should she care? He was not a part of her life. He had made that very clear!

"I'd better hurry," said Susan, dashing away.

Libby shook her head. Would she ever be happy again?

Snowball nickered and bobbed her head up and down as Libby walked slowly down the aisle.

"I forgot your treat," said Libby sadly. "I'm sorry." She wanted to rest her head against Snowball's neck and sob. Instead, she methodically carried grain to each horse, then let them out into the pen. Snowball neighed and kicked up her heels, then dashed around and around. "At least *she's* happy," Libby thought.

Libby picked up the barn cat and rubbed between his ears. "Did you find a big, juicy mouse for Christmas breakfast? I don't think I can eat at all. Mom is making breakfast for us now. How can I pretend to eat waffles this morning?"

Tears slipped down her cheeks, and she dropped the cat and rubbed them away. Why cry? It didn't do any good. Someday she would forget all about Scott Norris. She would think only about playing the piano the very best she could. She would be a famous concert pianist and Scott would be very sorry that he'd been mean to her.

The barn door opened and Libby turned in alarm to see Scott walking in. She stood rooted to the spot, unable to run away. Why hadn't he stayed away from her? He had only one more week here before he left. He could have stayed out of her way for a week.

He stopped in front of her and she sniffed hard. "I'm very sorry, Elizabeth," he said gently. "I keep hurting you and I'm sorry. Please forgive me."

She backed away until she bumped into a stall. "I can't," she whispered in agony.

"I don't blame you, but I need you to forgive me. I can't leave here knowing that I hurt you deeply." He walked along the aisle, then turned and stopped in front

106

of her. "I am proud that you love me. Someday maybe I will feel the same about you, but right now I see you as a young girl." He nodded and she caught back a sob. "You are young, but you know where you're going and you'll make it. I know you will."

She licked her dry lips. "You could make it, too, Scott." Oh, wouldn't she ever learn? Why couldn't she just keep her mouth shut? "I'm sorry."

"Don't be, Elizabeth." He pushed his hands into his jeans pockets and hunched his shoulders. "You are right. I have to do what is right for me. My parents can't choose my life for me. My sisters can't either. *I* must. If you want to know the truth, Elizabeth, I'm a little afraid."

Her eyes sparkled and she lifted her pointed chin high. "No, Scott, don't be! You can be a songwriter just as I can be a famous concert pianist and Jill can be a writer! You can be, Scott!"

He held her face between his hands and she almost melted with love for him. "You're a bright girl, Elizabeth. I don't think I will ever forget you."

"I will never forget you," she whispered. She knew love was shining from her eyes, but she didn't try to hide it.

He lowered his head and gently touched his lips to hers. He stepped back a little and smiled. "Merry Christmas, Elizabeth Gail Johnson, concert pianist!"

She tried to speak, but nothing came out. She watched as he turned and walked away. She touched her lips and could still feel his kiss.

The barn door closed and she rushed to it and opened it and watched as Scott strode across the yard toward the house. "I love you," she whispered. "I will love you forever!"

*If you've enjoyed the **Elizabeth Gail** series,
double your fun with these delightful heroines!*

Anika Scott

#1 The Impossible Lisa Barnes

#2 Tianna the Terrible

Cassie Perkins

#1 No More Broken Promises

#2 A Forever Friend

#3 A Basket of Roses

#4 A Dream to Cherish

#5 The Much-Adored Sandy Shore

#6 Love Burning Bright

You can find Tyndale books at fine bookstores everywhere.
If you are unable to find these titles at your local bookstore,
you may write for order information to:

**Tyndale House Publishers
Tyndale Family Products Dept.
Box 448
Wheaton, IL 60189**